A Piece of Her Soul

Serendipity, Indiana - Book Seven

by

Magdalena Scott

A Piece of Her Soul

© 2016 Magdalena Scott

ISBN-13: 978-0-9971922-7-8

Cover Art by Elusive Dreams Designs
Stock Art from DepositPhotos.com
Published by Jewel Box Books

Chapter One

"MOTHER FELL DOWN her basement steps. She's going to be okay. I just wanted you to know."

I'd been fixing dinner in my RV, but at my sister's words, all the air left my lungs. I shut off the gas burner, and collapsed into a captain's chair with my cell in hand. The chair started to spin.

"She's going to be okay—as in, she has broken bones that will mend? What?" I know my tone was less than sweet, but I'd been blindsided by Jen's news.

"Yes, that. One bone in her leg. And lots of bruises. She's in the hospital, and after that it's a rehab place, and then... Well, we're not sure yet. Marcus and I have discussed it—"

"You've discussed it with Mother, too, right?" Jen and her husband would try to do the best thing for

Mother. But she should make the decision for herself, if possible.

"Mother's not really able to talk about it now, Jacquie. She isn't herself yet. The meds." Jen sounded exhausted.

That's all I needed to hear. Mother had always been a rock—for many people, but particularly for me, the wayward daughter. When she got out of rehab, she'd be eager to get back to the home she loved, that she and Dad had built. If I could make it an easy, safe option, that's what I needed to do.

Until this accident she had been busy and vibrant, taking trips or doing projects with her best buddy, Lillian Standish. She made meals and delivered to folks who were ill or bereaved, volunteered at a couple of nonprofits in town, participated in at least one book club... I didn't know all of it, but I knew Mother wouldn't be ready to give up—or at least shouldn't be.

"Jen, I'm coming. I'll get out of here as quickly as possible, and start driving. When will she be released from rehab?"

"Around the first of October, the doctor says."

Her voice was strained. Did Jen doubt my sincerity after such a long absence?

Resolved, I made a mental inventory of the tasks I'd need to finish, avoiding a close scan of my paper calendar. My cat, Sam, jumped onto my lap, demanding to be stroked.

"October first," I repeated. "I can make that work. I'll be in Serendipity, stay with her so she can go home. At least—assuming you don't have a problem with that idea? I know you and Marcus have stuff going on, and I can be flexible."

I could *learn* to be, right? Flexibility was something I had always admired in others, though my version of it tended to be driven by a need to get *away* from a situation, not step *into* one. "Don't you think she'll do better in familiar surroundings?"

There was a long moment of silence. Then, "Yes, I do, and I was trying to figure out how to make it happen. I think you're right about coming home—it would be great medicine for her. You know how she feels about that house. I'm sure she'd love to have you with her, Jacquie." She paused again. "This is very generous. Umm... I'll let you surprise her when you get here."

Meaning, Jen wasn't sure quite I'd come through on the promise. I couldn't blame her for being cautious. If Mother got excited about me returning so she could be home, and then I didn't show up, that would stink, and Jen would be left playing clean-up.

I summoned a light tone. "Perfect, Jen. I love the idea of being a happy surprise for once. Thanks for calling. It means a lot that you thought of me, and let me know right away. Keep me updated, okay?"

"Yes. Sure, I will. And of course I thought of you. I think of you a lot, Jacquie. Miss you." I could imagine the look on her face. A little bit dazed by my stated intention. By the possibility of the absent sister showing up and doing the right thing.

If she only knew about my relationship with doing the right thing. She was better off thinking whatever she did about me.

"Great. If there's nothing else, I need to run for now, Jen."

But the truth was, I didn't need to run. I'd been

running for years, and it was time to do the opposite. I had felt pulled toward Serendipity for a while, and now there was no putting it off. I hoped I was strong enough to do what would be required of me there.

****

There was no doubt that the gossip tree of little Serendipity, Indiana would start buzzing with news of my reappearance, as soon as someone recognized me. I couldn't let myself care. My purpose wasn't to impress anyone or win a popularity contest, but to help Mother, and Jen.

On the other hand, what *I* needed right now was a nice, quiet cave to hide in. A cave that wasn't cold, damp, or dark, but well-lit and airy, with a lovely view of... Okay, not a cave. I could make do with an out-of-the-way camping spot for my RV van, with no close neighbors, and breathtaking scenery on every side. I needed a place to rest, and to heal.

Unlike Mother's injury, mine was invisible. And I intended to keep it a secret from everyone who wasn't already aware of it. My focus was on Mother, not myself.

To have an extended period of time with her would be a treat, in spite of the reason for it. As long as Mother and I were in her house together, or just around our family, I should be fine. But what about the proximity to so many people I'd known back in the day? I shivered at the possibilities.

A few years ago, in a fit of homesickness, I had considered a visit. I pressed Jen to tell me what people thought of my absence, and she finally conceded to my prodding.

"If you're not going to rest until you know, Jacquie, a lot of the town folks think you're an ungrateful egomaniac."

That hurt, but wasn't a surprise. "Oh, nice. Why did I ask?"

"Mmm-hmm. You know how people are."

"Sad to say, yes I do." The fact that I knew, much too intimately, how people are should have warned me off the question, and off of expecting to ever feel at home again in Serendipity.

Chapter Two

JEN GAVE ME frequent updates, and I phoned Mother every day, hoping to keep her spirits up. But my coming back was kept a secret between me, Jen, and Marcus. He sent me a text telling me how glad he was about my return. That Jen was looking forward to it like crazy, and Mother would be super excited. It was a nice message, but contained a statement between the lines: I needed to fulfill my promise, so I wouldn't hurt both of those special women. I sent him a quick text back.

Message received, loud and clear. (Smiley face.)

Jen found a great guy in Marcus. He was devoted to her, a wonderful dad to their children, and intensely loyal. He was also as good to Mother as a son would have been.

He managed to tolerate me, and I couldn't expect more.

The day I drove into town was weird. In this little place where people easily recognized each other by their vehicle, no one knew who was behind the wheel of the sleek, dark van with tinted windows and an out-of-state license plate. I came onto the square, navigated the roundabout, and found a parking space. Turning off the engine, I silenced Diana Krall's soothing jazz, took a steadying breath, and emerged into Serendipity.

The old hometown looked the same, but different. There were a couple of empty store fronts on the square, and several homes and businesses on the main drag that needed paint or other exterior upkeep. Serendipity was having a hard time entering the 21st century, even though the rest of the world had done so a decade and a half ago.

The bell jingled over the door of Emily's Dreams consignment shop as I entered, and a customer and the manager glanced at me. The manager—my sister—gasped, the customer looked confused by her reaction, and I avoided an introduction by stepping into the side room to browse. A few minutes later the bell jingled again, and Jen was in front of me.

"Jacquie. Wow. I...umm..."

I nodded. "You didn't think I'd really get here. I know."

She blushed, embarrassed by the truth, and a shy hand reached for mine. "But I'm so glad you made it."

I squeezed her hand, pulled her into a tight hug. "Me, too."

****

Jen gave me directions as I drove the van to the rehab place in New Albany. "It's been surreal making this trek to Meadowbrooke again," she said. "Marcus and I did it every day for such a long time, after Emily's wreck."

I should have made the connection to their daughter's recuperation, but hadn't. "I'm sure it's been tough on you guys. I guess your choice to move Mother here for her rehab must mean you think the place does good work."

"Yes, they're great. Still, I look forward to never seeing the inside of this place again." Her laugh sounded rusty.

"I'm sorry for the strain you've been under, Jen."

She pointed out the entrance door and I parked near it.

"It's okay," She said. "I'm used to it."

The truth hurt. "I wish I could have been here sooner."

She picked up her handbag from the floor by her feet, avoiding my eyes. "No one expected you to come and help out, Jacquie. We know your life is...complicated."

I locked the van as we walked toward the single-story brick building. "That's a good word for it. I'm glad to be able to help, you know. So many times, I wish I could have been here. I've missed so much."

"It's okay. We understand."

She wanted to, I knew. I closed my eyes against the memories of our issues in the past. If she was willing to set those aside, I could, too.

"At least, I'm here now," I said, brightly, for both our sakes. "It should be all good. The only thing I'm worried about is Mother's next-door neighbor. That's a complication I could do without."

Jen's brow furrowed. "I know. I thought about Nick when we hung up the phone that first day after Mother's accident. I hope it won't be too awkward for you. He's been good to her, if that helps at all."

"Right. She's told me, like a bazillion times, how Nick steps in when she's doing yard work, carries groceries if he sees her dragging in a bunch of stuff. He sounds like the perfect neighbor for a woman on her own."

The perfect neighbor for Mother, but having Nick next door was an unwanted reminder of the past, for me. I pushed the thought aside where I had tried to keep it ever since Jen's call. If I ran into Nick, which was almost certain, I could deal with it. I wasn't a young girl with a heart in danger of being broken. Nope. I was a woman who felt ancient before her time, with a heart that had nearly dried up from neglect and hopelessness.

"Who knows? Maybe nothing will happen with Nick." Jen said. "It may turn out to be a non-starter."

I managed a lame-sounding chuckle. "It always was."

She cringed. "Oops. Not the best way to phrase it. Anyway, if you want me or Marcus to talk to him, we will. I'd expect him to understand you don't want to see him."

I put an arm around her shoulders. "Thanks, but there's no need for you guys to do that. I'll handle whatever happens." It wouldn't be easy, but nothing in my life was simple.

We'd been speaking in low tones as we walked along the hall. Jen gestured at the door number I'd been looking for, and we paused briefly, before stepping into Mother's room together.

She looked tiny and frail, seated in a chair near the window, but her eyes brightened when she saw us. She smiled and clapped her hands together in delight. "Come over here and give me a hug and kiss, girls."

Jen and I exchanged a quick look at Mother's reaction, and did what we'd been told.

When Mother finally let go of the near choke-hold she had me in, I said, "You're not even surprised to see me."

"No. Why should I be? You forget that I know your heart, Jacqueline. Of course you wouldn't let me be a burden to your sister."

"Mother!" Jen's face turned pink. "You're not a burden. You could never be that."

"I know your heart too, Jennifer," she said. "You would do anything for me. I'm just glad you don't have to exhaust yourself further, on my account."

She still held my hand, and I wondered if she planned to let go any time soon. At least it was reassuring that her strength was good.

"So wonderful to have you home, Jacqueline." It wasn't home to me anymore, would never be that again, but pointing that out would only make us all feel bad.

Jen had brought an empty cardboard carton, and started to put loose items into it. "Jacquie came so you can go to your house instead of...you know...something else."

Mother nodded, having figured that out. "I've been eager to go home. Thank you, Jacqueline. I know this isn't easy for you." Her gaze shifted to Jen, and she grabbed her hand again. "I'll never forget all that you and Marcus have done for me, Jennifer. Where would I be without my girls?"

"Well, we're not going to find out any time soon." I kissed her cheek, extracted my hand, and checked the weight of a nearby suitcase. There were two of them, and a vase of flowers that might be left over from something I had sent. "Are you ready to bust out of this joint, Mother? The get-away car is waiting outside."

Her eyes sparkled. "Let's do it."

Chapter Three

MOTHER WAS FUSSING with tea and cookies in her cozy kitchen. Her movements were slow and cautious, but she often assured me that she didn't have pain. I had begged her not to do the staircases any time soon. Her apartment renters—one widow downstairs and one upstairs—could come to her, to pay rent, or to chat, as they occasionally did. If something in an apartment needed attention, Jen, Marcus, or I would deal with it, or we would call a professional. One day into our new living arrangement, and we were fine. My van was parked in her carport, and I was camping out in her spare bedroom-office.

"Jacqueline, I hope Serendipity will start to feel like home to you again, soon." Her gentle words wrapped me in a hug.

"That would be nice, but I don't expect it. I'll stay as long as you need me, Mother, but I'm not looking at this as permanent. Still, I appreciate your warm welcome, after...everything."

"Nonsense. You've always been welcome here, and you know it. We love you, honey." She reached across the table and squeezed my hand. "Please don't worry. Everything will work out. You'll see. I have an idea you'll be very happy in Serendipity this time. And I can't wait for you to meet little Isabel!"

I was looking forward to seeing my niece Emily and the baby, but long-term residence just wasn't in the cards. Not here, and not anywhere else. I stirred my tea and lifted the delicate cup to my lips, careful not to hurt Mother's feelings by scoffing at the idea that I would fit in. "Here's to new possibilities."

Mother raised her cup, too, and winked. "New possibilities."

****

A few days later, I set a hardy English ivy plant

onto the sunny window sill in the kitchen and stepped back, appraising it. *Just right*. A touch of green offers such hope for the future. At least that's what I've read.

Mother was napping, which had become her habit after lunch. I often took the quiet time to nap myself, do some online research for a future project, or take a walk in the city cemetery a couple of blocks away, where nobody would bother me. Being alone, or with one or two people at a time, was best for me. I had to maintain quiet if I was to recover my equilibrium. Otherwise I'd be no use to Mother.

When I left Atlanta and headed north, I felt ancient and depressed. But in just a few days here, my strength and energy had improved. I hoped it could last as long as Mother needed me, but knew better than to expect a long-term reprieve from the exhaustion.

I poured cider into a mug and nuked it. Pulling on a sweater, I went outside, where I curled up onto the glider. Sam jumped up next to me. I hadn't realized he had come out the front door too. That was Sam, though. He did pretty much what he wanted. As far as he was concerned, I was his slave. My purpose was to buy his favorite salmon cat food, supply fresh catnip upon request, and pet him endlessly. Other than that and an immaculate litter box, his requirements were few. I sipped cider and stroked his smooth, black coat.

He was adjusting well, considering he'd never spent extended time with Mother before, or lived with anyone but me since I rescued him as a tiny kitten, from an RV park trash can. When we first moved into Mother's house, I watched him closely to be sure he wouldn't rub against her legs as she walked and cause her to fall, but I should have realized he would sense her difficulties. Sam allowed Mother to pet him, and curled into her lap when she watched TV, but when she was walking, he stayed clear.

Feeling his weight shift, I looked down at him. He was sitting up straight, as if vigilant. Maybe he'd caught sight of a squirrel in one of the trees. "The season's changing. You'll like autumn, Sam. It's my favorite."

He made a sound that was not quite a purr.

The autumn color was just beginning. Soon the neighborhood would be festooned in bright yellows and vivid reds, some trees with both, which in the right light would make them look almost pink. The wind picked up and the color-tinged leaves fluttered. I shivered as a familiar feeling crept up my scalp. I was suddenly ice cold.

Shaking my head in a vain attempt to get rid of the awareness, I concentrated on enjoying the tangy cider, the fresh air, and the reassuring warmth of Sam's body next to me. We had things to look forward to. Halloween wasn't far away. Would Mother want to give out candy to the kids? If I stayed very long, I'd need some warmer clothes for an Indiana winter.

"Sam, you'll have to stay close to me when we're outdoors. Some people get weird about black cats this time of year." He looked up at me and yawned, signifying his boredom with my concern.

The feeling came over me again. The sensation of something ice cold creeping over my skin—up my neck, to my scalp, and back down again to the base of my spine.

No! This shouldn't be happening. I squeezed my eyes shut tight. Sam meowed plaintively. That was it, then. When Sam got in on it, I knew there was no ignoring the situation.

"Fine. Great." I opened my eyes, uncurled my legs and sat up straight, then turned in the direction I knew somebody was standing. I'd felt the presence as soon as the prickling sensation began.

A tall man was in the next yard, blatantly staring at me. *How rude*. Was that now the approved way to greet a neighbor in Indiana? Gritting my teeth, I stood, giving Sam a smooth caress.

"I'll just go see if it's something I can deal with quickly, shall I? Then it's salmon for you while I make some veggie soup for Mother and me." Sam meowed again and jumped off the glider, following as I crossed the yard to confront the stranger.

When I saw him more closely, my fear was confirmed. The years had changed him very little.

"Hi, Nick. Doing surveillance?"

His blue eyes had a glint, and a deep chuckle rumbled in his chest. But his smile was artificial.

He gave me a slow, thorough appraisal from head to toe. In spite of our history, my pulse quickened.

It had been a while since I'd had strength for any close relationships, let alone a romantic one.

"Hi, Jacquie. I heard you were here."

I shrugged. "News travels, as usual."

"I never expected you to come back to Serendipity," he said.

I crossed my arms over my chest, aware of the body language signal it sent. "Neither did I, but plans change."

"I guess."

"Who would have expected *you* to move here, Nick?"

He tipped his head in assent. "Yeah. Not me. Not back then, anyway."

This conversation needed to end. I didn't want to say something ugly to Nick, because Mother was a fan of his. But I had no use for him. Lucky for me, the feeling was mutual.

"Anyway, I'll be here for a while, Nick, so you don't need to come over and check on Mother. Don't need to do yard work, carry groceries, whatever."

He frowned, and his eyes looked darker because

his brows shaded them from the weakening October sunlight. "I care about Reba, so I'll help her out as I see fit. The family has never minded that. They've been grateful."

I shrugged, noting the fact that *the family* obviously didn't include me. But I didn't want to let on that anything he could say or do would have an impact on me. "I can't speak for Jen and Marcus, or for Mother. Just know that we've got enough going on, and don't need any complications. I'm here for Mother. You're not needed. So if you stay out of my way while I'm in town, everything will be peachy." I squeezed out a bitter grin. "I'd think you'd be glad to do that, considering."

Nick ran a hand through his dark hair, mussing it into something appropriate for a model in a GQ photo shoot. He was always handsome, but this bed-head look sent my thoughts in a direction I had to jerk them back from.

"I hear you talking, Jacquie, but as usual you're not telling the whole story."

I swallowed a reply. An escalation would serve

no purpose, except to make our next few weeks as neighbors even less pleasant.

I gestured at the three-story Victorian home behind him. "So. Your aunt and uncle left you the house. Nice."

"Yeah." He slid his hands in the front pockets of his jeans. "Georgia and Ed didn't have kids, you know. But I was surprised when the lawyer got in touch with me."

He had liked Serendipity more than I, but never expressed an interest in living the small town life on a permanent basis. "Because you didn't have any inclination to move here."

He nodded. "Right. But it worked out. The job in town, plus some stuff going on where I was living. Everything kind of fell into place, so it made sense to come here after all." His eyes had gone from suspicious to sad while he was talking.

"Hmm." I didn't want to hear his story, didn't want to know what was going on with him now, or what had happened to nudge him into relocating. Every second I talked with Nick, some of the peaceful feeling

I'd begun to develop slipped away from me.

"Guess you should have expected things to fall into place, Nick. After all, Serendipity is more than a little famous for coincidences that *aren't*." I thought of what had happened to Emily after her wreck, and the stories of the Standish family. Lillian Standish was Mother's best friend, and whatever was big news in Lillian's world made it into Mother's conversations with me. Now that Emily had married into the Standish family, the bond had strengthened.

Nick smiled and his face became even more handsome. I hated him for it. "As you might guess, the gossip tree has been whispering about you. I wanted to see first-hand."

"Oh, the dreaded gossip tree. How I've missed it." I smiled, hoping I looked amused, instead of worried about what kind of details the gossip tree might get hold of, and spread. "So, let me guess what you've heard. Hmm. *Reba's black-sheep daughter is back in town. That girl was always trouble. She's just here to prey on her mom while she's weak.* Or maybe this: *David and Emily Standish had better lock up that sweet baby of theirs. No telling what her weird Aunt Jacquie might have in store.*"

His grin turned more genuine.

"Actually, just the one about you being the black-sheep daughter. I'll keep an ear out for the weird Aunt Jacquie comment, though. That one's classic."

"You wouldn't say that if you were the target of gossip."

He frowned. "Come on, Jacquie. You know everybody's the target of gossip in Serendipity. It's the official pass time."

I picked Sam up, started to stroke him, needing to feel his warm body next to mine. The chill of awareness wasn't abating. "Well, just so you know, I'm not going to do anything worthy of gossip. I'm here for Mother, as I said, and I'll be keeping my head down. You won't have any problem with wild parties next door, for instance."

"I'm relieved to hear that. Considering my job."

The stupid small talk made me want to scream. If he would just stop needing...whatever it was.

While we talked, I was trying to figure out why

I was getting those signals that ruled my life. These were stronger than I'd ever experienced. Yet I didn't sense anything from Nick but relaxed composure, and the inclination to push any buttons of mine he could find. Often I could read an intense need in a person's eyes. The strength of my sensations said this was an intense one…but he sure didn't show it. I didn't want to delve into what was going on with Nick Marshall. He was the last person in the world I wanted to be responsible for.

He smiled at me again.

"Could I tempt you, Jacquie?"

Sam jumped out of my arms.

"Tempt?"

He shook his head. "That's disappointing. You don't even look the slightest bit shocked. Okay, I'm talking about food. I'm a mean hand with a gas grill, and your mom loves a good steak." He chuckled as Sam pounced on a flurry of leaves stirred by the breeze. "Season's ending soon, you know. How about a steak and potato on the grill to cheer Reba up? I guess you can consider it a welcome home, if you want."

"A grudging welcome, you mean."

Frown lines appeared between his brows. "Let's bury the hatchet—not in my back, please—for Reba's sake. If you keep her away from everybody *you* don't like, she won't get out at all."

"That's an awful thing to say."

"Deny it. Or better yet, get Reba out for some fresh air and let me cook dinner. You can drive her over if you're concerned about her walking across the yard."

My blood pressure was rising. "You're awfully sure of yourself, Nick. I guess you think you can order everybody around, but that won't work with me." He was a police officer, his childhood dream-job, and Mother said the citizens thought the world of him. That was typical—he had a lifetime of getting what he wanted. "You're doing it, you know. Trying to take over. This is what I expected from you."

The frown deepened. "Reba is a special lady. And yes, I'm protective of Serendipity, and its people. Part of the job."

Part of the man, too. Setting aside my well-founded dislike of Nick, I could tell the protective spirit was all around him. He would always take care of people, especially those he cared about. Who might that be? A wife? Kids? No, Mother would have told me news like that, and I wasn't getting any sense of a romantic relationship. The guy was one of the easiest reads I'd done in years, but I still wasn't getting an idea of what he needed. Until I took care of Nick's needs, I knew that the niggling feeling would crawl over me whenever he was near, teasing and taunting.

I felt my face go red as I thought of the physical needs Nick Marshall would have. Well, those were not my problem. Even if I was attracted to him, which I wasn't—anymore—my intervention in lives was never physical. So if Nick needed *that*, I couldn't help him with it.

Sam rubbed against my ankle, leaned on me, purring. I jerked my mind out of the gutter and frowned up at Nick.

"I told Mother I'd make vegetable soup for dinner."

"As I said, Reba likes a good steak. Check with her, will you? She has my number."

He winked at me and went home, rustling the few dry leaves on the lawn as he walked. When he went inside, I turned my back, embarrassed that I'd been staring.

"Come on, Sam. Let's go in. Man, you just don't know who's going to show up and ruin your day, do you?"

Later, when Mother awakened from her nap and was in the living room, I told her about the invitation. "A cookout would be such fun, wouldn't it? I'm so glad Nick asked. You must call and say *yes*, Jacqueline. And ask what you can bring." She scrolled through her cell contacts and read off his number.

I didn't make a note of his number, didn't want the man in my cell records, or anywhere else in my life. But her face had lit up when I'd mentioned the invitation, so I needed to set my own feelings aside, like the good daughter I was trying to be.

"Why don't *you* call him, Mother? Just tell him I'll bring you over whatever time he wants." I hated giving in to him, but it was her choice. If it was possible, I'd skip the festivities.

"Oh, I'm not going. I feel tired this afternoon, honey. If you just make me that soup, I'll be fine. You go on over to Nick's and have a good time."

"No. Absolutely not. I'm here to—"

"To take care of me. Yes, I realize. And you're doing a marvelous job. I feel loved and pampered. But sweetheart, I need my space once in a while. I'm used to living alone, remember? Having you with me is a delight, but I think we both should take occasional breaks. Make sense?"

"Yes, it does. But still, I don't..."

She leaned into the couch cushion, looked even more tired. "Please. Go next door, get to know Nick again. Heal those old wounds you're guarding, Jacquie. He's a wonderful friend and neighbor, and Serendipity is fortunate he came here to live. Give the man a chance. Who knows what might happen?"

I knew what would happen. I'd get a reading on Nick, figure out what his problem was, and help him find his answer. Then he'd have a better life, and I'd be exhausted from the process. But Mother was looking up at me, expectation in her eyes, along with the weariness that had come over her during the conversation.

"Okay. Give me the number again." Grinding my teeth, I put Nick's info into my cell phone. I knew the purpose of having me call was so he would have my number. Mother was a transparent matchmaker. She just didn't realize she was working on an impossible case this time.

****

Nick answered on the second ring.

"Hi. It's Jacqueline. Mother wants to stay home and eat soup, but she's encouraging me to be sociable. So if the offer is still open, what may I bring? A bottle of wine?"

Yikes. Where had that come from? "Veggies and dip?" I amended.

"Sure. Wine would be different—I mean, good. But we're good on food. Around seven okay for you?"

Around seven would give me plenty of time to cook and serve Mother's dinner and clean it up, then fret and pace before presenting myself next door, to learn what it was Nick Marshall needed in order to get his life on track. And, oh yeah—I needed to hit the grocery and buy a bottle of wine.

"Okay," I said, and ended the call.

I left Mother in the living room, smiling as she paged through magazines. Curled next to her, Sam purred, watching the colorful images go past. Nice picture of domestic bliss, while I went into the kitchen and made a good deal of noise with my vegetable soup project. After a few minutes, I toned it down, realizing I was taking out my frustration on Mother's pots and pans.

Maybe Nick's guard would be down this evening, and he'd be pleasant instead of himself. My experience with him was that he had a smart mouth and a razor-sharp wit that could cut deep. Back in ancient history, he and I had been close. We were friends, heading toward something more. At least, that's what I had thought.

The *something more* seemed to be unattainable for me—back then, and even more so now. In the last few years I'd had trouble even making friends, because I was always too tired and overwhelmed by trying to fulfill the needs of those around me.

That is my gift—determining what is lacking in someone's life. The piece that was missing from each person's soul was attainable, but many people these days couldn't find it on their own.

Chapter Four

WHEN I WAS twelve years old, I realized I was different from Jen and my friends, because I could sense things about people. Until then I'd thought everyone could do what I did, but just didn't talk about it. The day I realized the truth, we were at my grandparents' house.

My dad and grandfather were watching a ball game on TV, Mom and Grandma were in the sewing room working on a quilt. Jennifer was home from college for the weekend, bored to death being stuck with me, but not interested in the ball game, or in trying to make the tiny stitches that were required for quilting. This was before cell phones, so she couldn't just retreat into the digital world.

Jen and Marcus were dating, and when he and

his younger brother Jamison came to the house to return a library book to Jen—haha, as if anyone believed that excuse for an exchange of longing looks—I stepped onto the porch with her, hung around while the three of them talked. It was no surprise that she wanted me to go inside and give them some privacy, but I took pride in my status as Pesky Kid Sister. After a while, the boys got in Marcus's car and drove away.

Jen sighed as if she'd just had an audience with the man of her dreams, which, looking back, she had. There was a silly smile on her face when she floated across the porch floor and melted onto the swing. I walked over to her, wondering why she seemed so out of it. When she didn't look at me, I said, "Marcus needs to stand up to Jamison, or he'll never be taken seriously."

Nudged out of her trance, Jen looked at me, suspicion in her eyes. "What?"

"Marcus lets his little brother push him around. If he keeps acting that way, he won't get what he wants in life. I'd think you might want him to do that, Jen, if you plan on marrying him." I shrugged, and went into the house. Jen's mouth was hanging wide open.

In a few minutes she was in spilling it all to Mother and Grandma. Once she'd finished, Mother got Jen calmed down, told her she needed help with some reorganization of Grandma's pantry. While they were doing that, Grandma gave me *the talk*.

She told me that I had the same gift she did. She said when she discovered hers, there weren't a lot of people in need of it. As time passed, though, more people were unable to find that missing piece without help.

So many people live in quiet desperation, to paraphrase Thoreau. They're on a meaningless treadmill and don't realize it, don't understand why they feel unfulfilled. How surprised they would be to learn it's because each soul literally has a small hole. "Original equipment with a built-in flaw," as Grandma often referred to it.

For those who don't find the missing piece on their own, the task—Grandma's, mine, and whoever else has the gift—is to discover what each person's soul needs, and then surreptitiously lead them to it. Payment for the work is the glowing smile on each recipient's face.

Grandma told me, her tone more serious than I had ever heard her use, "No one is to know what we do. Telling others would serve no purpose other than to expose us to ridicule, and possibly jeopardize our ability to be of service."

Since I was just a kid when this happened, Grandma decided Mother needed to know. So at least I didn't feel completely alone when, during my eighth grade year, Grandma died. As soon as I was old enough, I left Serendipity, trying to escape the memories. Bewildered stares of those I'd tried to help when I was young and awkward, and the whispering behind my back at the results of the coping methods I eventually fell into.

Similar to freaking Jen out with my observation about Marcus, I managed to set myself apart as an oddity, while trying to do the work Grandma didn't have time to prepare me for. I was too young and inexperienced, and had a tendency to say the wrong things. All of that added up to a big fat negative.

Being called *Geoffrey and Reba's black sheep daughter* is probably not the worst of it, but I was glad not to know more. Once I left Serendipity, I worked my way into a career that suited me and my gift. To the casual observer, I'm just a self-employed travel writer who specializes in quiet, undiscovered places. I make some money, and usually don't need to remain too long in any location. Wherever I go, I find people who need my help. I am able to build respites into my schedule, which is important because the gift takes a lot of energy. Living in a van-sized RV means I can park anywhere and not be conspicuous. Because I can live off the grid for a few days, it's possible to get away from it all.

The RV had broken down while I was traveling through Atlanta, and I was stuck there while a part was shipped. Even that short stay in the city had been maddening—always surrounded by people, my gift was on call 24/7. Walking down a busy sidewalk was like navigating a series of emotional typhoons. So many unfulfilled people, so much need. I'd been desperate to get on the road, and to a quiet place. So Jen's call, and

Mom's need for some support, had come at the perfect time. If I worked it right, my visit could serve a secondary purpose of allowing me time to rest and recover.

But with the Nick problem, it seemed my stay in Serendipity wasn't going to be a respite after all.

Chapter Five

I CLUTCHED A bottle of red wine by its neck and stepped out Mom's back door, crossing the short distance to Nick's back deck. He walked outside as I approached. Tall, dark, and handsome—it should be illegal, especially in law enforcement personnel.

I gave myself a mental shake. Sure, he was good looking—yet another example of the fact that life isn't fair. He deserved to have a big, ugly wart on the end of his nose, preferably with a wiry black hair growing out of it. That would be a nice warning for all women to stay out of his reach, the jerk. And maybe he should have incurable halitosis, too. Bad breath that wouldn't go away would be a nice addition to the wart.

He was smiling at me, wart-less nose and all, as

if he was glad to be entertaining me, instead of just fulfilling that disgusting *perfect neighbor* role for Mother.

I climbed the deck steps. If I didn't manage to keep my mind on the *job*, we'd never get this soul repaired. Would it be so wrong to leave him with that gaping hole when I drove away from Serendipity in a few weeks? I knew Grandma would have had an answer to that question. But she had barely known Nick. She'd died about five years before he'd done as bad, or worse, to me, that summer after I graduated high school.

Then it hit me again. The creeping cold up my neck and scalp, and down my spine, that was more intense than I remembered it ever being. I shivered inside my heavy Georgia State sweatshirt, wondering how dorky I would look if I pulled up the hood for more warmth. Pretty dorky, I guessed, and snugged it closer to my neck instead.

"You're going to have to stop doing that, you know." Nick set a tray next to his grill, crossed his arms over his chest and shook his head at me.

"Um...stop doing what?" Freezing to death from the inside out on a slightly cool October night? Ogling bad-news hunks? Visualizing dermatological yuckiness, just for spite?

His eyebrows rose in surprise at my cluelessness. "Wearing the wrong sweatshirt. You'll need some cream and crimson in this part of the world. You do remember this is IU country?" He turned aside, set thick steaks onto the hot grill next to a couple of foil-wrapped packages.

I sighed and tried to relax. No way could I concentrate on Nick if I kept thinking about...well, Nick...but in the wrong way. I used my right hand to pry my left hand off the wine bottle I'd been clutching.

"Right, I do remember that. Jen is a Bloomington grad, after all."

And I would have been one, too, if I hadn't left the area in such a hurry. Several seconds passed when I couldn't think of anything to add. I pointed at the packets on the grill, desperate for a topic to take my mind off being near Nick, coupled with the sensations that wouldn't leave me alone. "Doesn't look like baked potatoes."

"Changed my mind. Chef's prerogative." Another of those killer smiles, and, wouldn't you know, I didn't get a whiff of any nasty breath. "I thought we'd have some carrots, onion, and peppers in with the potatoes. I cut 'em all up and used my special seasoning. You'll like it."

He was self-assured in his cooking, too. Of course.

Conversation was slightly less awkward as he talked about the little town, his most interesting cases, some of the colorful people in the area. I remembered a few of the names, but most were unfamiliar. In spite of myself, I laughed more that night than I had in months. As I stood on the bottom step of his deck, preparing to leave, a weird, twisted portion of my psyche wanted Nick to pull me into his arms and kiss me. That was out of the question, and a bad idea on so many levels. But for a moment I couldn't remember any of them. It didn't happen, of course. We said good night, and I left. By the time I walked into Mother's house, I had my head screwed on straight again.

Later, after I had given Mother the shorthand version of the evening (while she grinned like the Cheshire cat) and got her settled in bed, I lay in the dark in the guest room and thought about what had transpired.

Nick was a tough one to figure out. He was happy and mostly satisfied with his life, as far as I could tell. But the strength of my sensations told me I was missing something major. I wondered if my personal feelings for him were affecting my ability to help. Did it work that way? The only person I could have asked that question of was Grandma.

I had never run up against a situation in which the subject of my attention was someone I had strong feelings for. Of course, my strong feelings were negative, not that ridiculous dreamy-eyed l-u-v type of love I'd felt back in high school. After all this time, my feelings shouldn't be strong at all, one way or another. I should be able to look at Nick, or think about him, and have no more response than I would for any other person.

But since I wasn't living in a perfect world, I'd

have to do my best with what I had. It seemed my plan to lay low here in Serendipity had changed into an assignment of the most difficult case I'd ever come up against.

Chapter Six

ONE BRIGHT, CRISP morning, Mother and I got into my van and went to visit Emily. My niece had been keeping her daughter home, recovering from a chest cold that nobody wanted Mother to catch. When the doctor gave Isabel a clean bill of health, we set up a time to go see her.

"This will be such fun." Mother fidgeted in her seat like an excited three-year-old. "You haven't been to the tree farm in eons. Emily is looking forward to seeing you, and little Isabel is enchanting."

"Not that you're prejudiced at all."

She laughed. "Of course not."

Her voice reflected off the glass of her window. Turning, I saw she was avidly watching the scenery. I needed to get her out more often so she didn't get bored. I was trying to make sure she was safe, but couldn't bubble-wrap her and keep her in the house all the time.

If I was honest, I was trying just as hard to keep *myself* safe.

I turned into the Christmas tree farm's long drive, which curved among stands of evergreens of different heights. We passed a Craftsman-style house on the right.

"That's Carla's, you know. She's married now, to Jared Barnett. Katie and Miles adore her."

I'd heard the names, but other than Carla, whom I last saw when I was a teenager, didn't know any of them.

"Katie is a darling. She's in high school now—just amazing how grown up she is. Miles is nine. He and Matthew are best friends."

"And Matthew is Jim and Melissa's son." I had a sketchy drawing of the Standish family tree in my head, though the story of Matthew's place on the tree was still almost unbelievable.

"Yes, that's right. I shouldn't throw a lot of names around, and I try not to. You'll see everyone in time."

Maybe. But once I was satisfied Mother was able to be on her own, this van and I would be on our way out of town. Serendipity was my past, and my present, but not my future. As always for me, the future was a hazy, theoretical place in the distance. I had no idea what it looked like, or how I might get there. Some nights that fact kept me awake for hours. How delightful it would be to live a life like Mother's. Everything and everyone she cared about was in Serendipity. She had a full, enjoyable routine of events, and was open to new opportunities for fun when they presented themselves. In some ways, she seemed younger than I.

Like that cookout at Nick's. I had an idea she had participated in his outdoor entertaining efforts numerous times, and that she had reciprocated. I remembered her telling me about the annual neighborhood cookout, which Nick, when his year came around, took his turn in hosting. She'd made a big deal of telling me about it.

Imagine, a single man confident enough to host the whole group—a handful of widows, couples of all ages, and a passel of kids. Not every man would be willing to take on such a task. But Nick's special.

Sure, he was special. He was an especially bad memory. And he was especially a thorn in my side right now.

I pulled my mind back to the tree farm, and Mother. No amount of wishing for normalcy like hers would make a whit of difference in the strangeness, and the constant travel, of mine. The fact that Nick was here could not matter to me, on a personal level. He was just another client who didn't realize he needed my services.

After passing the big farm house where Jim, Carla, David, and Francie Standish had grown up, and where Francie and husband Brad now lived, we veered east and up another hill to the ranch-style house that was David and Emily's. My niece had seen us approaching, and was waiting outside the front door. A young boy stood next to her, holding the baby.

The boy handed Isabel to Mother for a cuddle of greeting, before I helped her out.

"I'm Matthew," he said, eyes smiling up into mine. "Isabel is my cousin, because our dads are brothers."

I shook his hand. "I'm happy to meet you, Matthew. I'm Jacqueline. You can call me Jacquie if you want." I gestured to Mother. "Reba is my mother, and Jennifer is my sister. So that makes Emily my niece." I watched him trying to process the information.

"Or we could just say we're all family," I said, and everyone laughed.

Emily gave me a hug. "Aunt Jacquie, it's great to see you. I'm glad Matthew was here to meet you. He's a huge help to me."

Matthew beamed. "Uncle David is gone during the week, so I come over to make sure everything is okay. It's just part of being a family."

My talking about family, and Matthew's version of being on the spot and participating in each other's daily events, were such different things. If not for Mother's efforts, I'd have been much more out of touch. Thank goodness she always arranged a family reunion, and most of the time there was a near-perfect attendance. Wherever I was living at the time, she'd find a hotel with a small meeting room, and she, Jen and Marcus and their kids—plus, since Emily's marriage, David Standish, would rent rooms. We'd have a long weekend of talking, laughing, eating at interesting restaurants, and sight-seeing.

Emily and David hadn't attended this year, because Isabel was brand new, and they were concerned about taking her on a long car trip. I heard about her throughout our reunion, and had seen loads of phone pictures, but now, when Emily handed me the tiny bundle, and I looked down into the face of my (gasp) great-niece, I had a new understanding of the term *love at first sight*.

I don't know how long I stood there on the front porch staring down at the beautiful child, marveling at the way she grasped my finger with one delicate hand, and inhaling her sweet baby scent. I finally came out of my trance when Isabel yawned, and her entire face contorted comically. I laughed, and the others joined in.

"Sorry, we don't have to stand here," I said. "I forgot you all existed."

"We're good," Emily said, pulling a chair nearer. "Here you go, Gran. Whenever you need it, okay?"

"Thank you, dear. Being out here on this gorgeous day makes me feel even better. Jacqueline has been taking wonderful care of me." She gazed out at the panoramic view of the Christmas tree farm. "This is such a lovely spot, Emily. I know I say that every time I visit, but it's true."

Emily slipped her hand into Mother's, and looked out, too. "I don't get tired of the view, no matter how many times I see it. This time of year, as the leaves change on all the surrounding farms, our acres of evergreens seem even greener." She shook her head. "It's hard to believe tree season starts in just a few weeks."

I looked down at the baby. "Tree season. What do you think of that, Miss Isabel?" She seemed to listen, her eyes wide as she watched my face. "I remember coming here with my parents and big sister to get our Christmas tree every year. You're a very lucky girl, you know."

Mother was inspecting the three-jack o'lantern family displayed on a stand. "Yes, Isabel is fortunate in many ways. And she's having her first Halloween with a great big celebration on her own farm. What fun that will be." She lowered herself into the chair Emily had provided, and I relinquished Isabel to her great-grandmother.

"Oh? What's going on here for Halloween?" I asked.

Matthew's face lit up. "Trunk or treat! I'm going to be Batman."

Emily laughed. "Yes, he is. I haven't seen the costume yet, but I hear it has muscles and everything."

Matthew nodded. "I wanted Miles to be Robin, but he said *no*. He wants to be Superman." He lifted his hands helplessly. "What are you gonna do?"

Emily smiled, and touched his head lovingly. It was clear there was a special connection between these two. "Francie thought of Trunk or Treat as another opportunity for families to come out and enjoy the tree farm. Since Halloween's door-to-door candy tradition has been evolving in recent years, why not, right?"

I stood in a sunbeam, enjoying its warmth on my face in spite of the breeze. "I've heard of a trunk or treat, but not in a location like this. How will it work?"

Emily looked almost as excited as Matthew. "Basically, a bunch of folks will dress up, decorate their trucks or cars, fill them with candy and other fun treats, and park them around the farm. When the kids and their parents get here, we'll give out maps and let them trudge off, trying to get to all the places on the map."

"That sounds fun."

Emily nodded. "The city has hosted it downtown in the past, but Jared Barnett keeps telling us we should change things up when we can. Francie wants to try new stuff on the farm, and this seemed a good fit."

"Harry would have been so proud of her for keeping up tradition, yet also being creative," Mother said. "I know Lillian is."

For years, three of the Standish siblings lived in their own homes on the tree farm. When their mother decided she needed to step down from the management position she had inherited from her husband when he died, the non-resident, Francie, offered to step up and take over the day to day running of the farm. She and husband Brad moved to Serendipity from their long-time home in Florida. I could imagine it was a major culture shock for Brad, but found myself envying Francie's ability to return to her roots when she wanted to.

"I heard about Lillian having a granny-pod installed behind the main house. How's that working out?" I asked.

"Really well," Emily said. "She loves the small, easy-to-clean space, and is so agreeable with whatever Francie wants to do at the main house. Lillian is an inspiration to me." She looked lovingly at my mother—her grandmother—who was paying little if any attention to us while she whispered and cooed to Isabel. "Lillian and Gran. I hope I'll be as cool as they are when I get to be their age."

"That's a worthwhile goal," I said.

We stayed at Emily's for a couple of hours, and when Isabel lay down for her nap, Matthew said his good-byes. Mother, Emily, and I had tea on the porch, with the nursery monitor at hand.

If only everyone was as happy and content as my niece, and my mother. I knew it wasn't because they had monetary wealth. It was because they had made the conscious choice to be happy.

For years I'd been trying to help people find what was missing from their lives, and without fail, the things they sought couldn't be purchased with dollars. The sense of peace that lay over our afternoon at the tree farm was a palpable thing, and I wished, as I often did, that more folks could let go of the belief that they had to constantly strive for more, bigger, shinier, newer. When they had those goals in mind, they tended to rush, constantly dissatisfied, right past the beauty of daily life.

My observation was that, in most instances, they already had enough to be happy. As far as I could tell, all that was required for happiness was a place to live, food, clothing, and meaningful relationships. Anything beyond that was just extra. But in the headlong rush to get *more*, the average person didn't recognize that having *enough* was, in fact, better.

That night as I lay in bed and remembered the special time at Emily's home, I recalled my musings, too. What about myself? I was satisfied with my life, because I had to be. Circumstances kept me from settling in one place for long, but I had learned to adjust. I loved to travel, and travel writing earned me enough money to live on. While I did my official career, my unofficial one was always in the wings, swooping down on me at unexpected times.

Never as unexpected as my interaction with Nick, though. I really wanted to get his situation dealt with, so I could enjoy my time in Serendipity. Mother was stronger and more confident each day, and before long—perhaps by Halloween—she'd be fine on her own, and wouldn't need me here. I didn't have the option of coming home as Francie had done, and fitting into the life of the community. It might be tempting to grow complacent and comfortable in my old hometown, but history had shown that if I started to settle in too much, I'd soon be in the midst of additional demands on my gift.

I couldn't afford for that to happen here. Sure, I could deal with the task and move on, but in my wake would be questions about what had happened, with Mother or Jen left to deal with the gossip. I couldn't do that to them, and not to Emily either. After hearing what had transpired when she ran her little consignment store, I knew Emily had a touch of the gift herself. Thank goodness it didn't seem to interfere with her life as it did with mine. Or to be more correct, my gift *ran* my life.

Grandma hadn't warned me about that, back when she explained the gift to me. She hadn't made it sound like a big burden at all, but a positive thing. Sometimes I wondered if I was handling it wrong, but there was nobody to ask.

Chapter Seven

MOTHER NEEDED A few errands done, and since the weather was beautiful, I walked the three blocks to the town square with her list. The cool air was refreshing, and an overnight rain had changed the scent wafting to my nostrils from leaves on the grass and sidewalks. I remembered this smell, associated it with raking leaves, going trick-or-treating. It was funny how many things came back to me here in Serendipity. Memories I didn't realize I even had now popped into mind, cued by something as simple as a fragrance.

I stopped in at the consignment store to see Jen, but she gestured at me helplessly, busy helping a couple of ladies who seemed to be from out of town and interested in discussing their purchases as well as the town's history. I signaled to her that I'd try back later, and went to the pharmacy to pick up the medicine refill order Mother had phoned in. The pharmacist and I had been in Girl Scouts together back in the day, and handed me the white sack marked *Charged.*

I marveled silently at the intricacies of small town life.

Next was a trip to the bank to cash a check for Mother. I wasn't sure how that would work, but after looking at the name plate, recognized the teller, Stacy, as a classmate of Jen's. After I introduced myself, she remembered me, and said her mother and mine were in a book club together. While she chatted and counted out money, I realized her soul was hurting. Her smile was pleasant, but her eyes sad, with dark circles under them. A vision of a man flashed into my mind, and when I picked up the envelope of money, I noted the wide indentation on the ring finger of Stacy's left hand.

I thanked Stacy, and departed. I'd need to find out more, but it looked as if her husband had left her. How to help? I couldn't ignore the sadness of her eyes, even if I was trying to avoid bringing attention to myself. I'd just have to be super careful.

My next stop was at the county treasurer's office, to pay Mother's fall installment on property tax. For this, she had given me another check, and again the transaction was simple because one of the employees went to the same church as Mother, and knew I was in town helping out. Besides, she said, why would anybody fake a check to pay property taxes?

On my way down the limestone steps of the castle-like courthouse, I met a beautiful woman with long, sleek, dark hair. She looked at me once, squinted in concentration, and then stopped, smiling at me.

"Jacquie. It's wonderful to see you!" She held out her hand. "Carla Standish."

"Oh, sure. You haven't changed at all, Carla."

Her head went back as she laughed—a musical sound. "That isn't true, but let's keep telling ourselves these little lies as long as we can. Actually, I'm married now, so the last name is Barnett."

"Yes, so I heard. And you have step-kids, right?"

"A girl in high school, Katie, and Miles is in

elementary. They're such joys, as is their father." She blushed a little. "I'd love for you to come out to the house some evening. You and Reba, I mean, if you can manage it. Mom is gone right now, and then we're hosting a community event at the farm, but after that, we'll have a reunion. Would that be good?" Her face clouded as she waited for my reaction.

"I'd love that, and I know Mother will."

Her smile returned. "Wonderful. So, are you settling into Serendipity all right? I know it's a massive change—from anywhere else. I travel quite a bit for work, and it always takes me a day or so to get back into the small town mindset. Much as I love living here, some facets of it can be exasperating."

"I'm good so far. Nothing exasperating." *Except this very awkward thing with Nick Marshall. And now Stacy...* "Everyone's been very nice."

Today was my first trip out on my own, and I was almost regretting it. Thank goodness, Carla was full of happiness, but I was sure anyone would have known that. It didn't take a special gift to see love written all over a face, as it was on Carla's. I wished again that I could be settled quietly into a simple life. Carla had said, and I knew from things Mother told me, that Carla was gone quite often with her dressmaking career. So she wasn't the typical happy homemaker of Serendipity. Maybe nobody like that even existed. Emily's husband traveled all week, and was home on weekends.

I shivered as a familiar feeling crept up my scalp. I was suddenly ice cold.

Carla touched my arm. "Are you okay, Jacquie? You look like you've just seen a ghost."

I managed a smile. "I'm good. Just remembered I have a lot to take care of. So...I'd better move on. Great to see you, Carla. Let us know on that get-together. Mother will love it!"

I would endure it because I needed to, though an event surrounded by Standish family members should be okay, if Emily, Matthew, and Carla were indicators.

Carla went up the steps to make her own property tax payment, I turned to go, and nearly ran into Nick.

He caught me by the upper arms, or I might

have toppled over.

"Whoa, now. What's your rush, Jacquie? You just rob a bank?"

Where his hands were on my jacket sleeves, my flesh was searing. I shrugged hard, and he got the hint, let go.

My heart was beating like the percussion section of the marching band at football game halftime I'd heard from Mother's open kitchen window a couple of Fridays ago. To avoid his eyes and attempt to recover my composure, I pulled Mother's list—the one I had already completed—out of my pocket.

"Hmm. Bank robbery isn't among my errands today. Just hurrying to get out of everybody's way. Seems to be a lot of excitement about paying property taxes."

He glanced around at the limestone staircase which was empty except for us, then looked straight into my eyes, since I was on the step above him.

"Right. It's a favorite local celebration. Notice the festival atmosphere. I'm here on official business, though. Clerk's office."

That's when I let myself take a good look at it. *The uniform.* They always gave me a fluttery feeling, but oh my word, Nick Marshall in his not-that-flashy police uniform was a bigger *wow* than I'd expected. Not that I'd spent any time wondering what he would look like in his uniform. Or, you know, out of it. I swallowed hard, hoping I wouldn't choke on the overload of saliva that had appeared in my mouth.

"You're staring, Jacquie."

I nodded and closed my eyes, taking a few seconds to try the meditation that sometimes calms me in emotional-overload situations. When I opened them again, I was struck by the unmistakable wash of concern on his face.

"Hey. Are you okay?"

The same question Carla had asked, and the answer was *no*, though I had to say otherwise.

"Yes. Fine. I guess I'm a little tired."

He nodded. "Sure. You have a lot on your plate. Anything I can help with?"

The insistent cold was traveling up and down my spine. I didn't want to be near Nick another moment, having these intense sensations. Yet I knew the only way to end them was to deal with whatever his problem was. Even if I could avoid Nick for my remaining time in Serendipity, for Mother's sake I should try to assure that her beloved neighbor was one hundred percent. My mind raced, in an effort to grab the right words and tone of voice, to present a little white lie.

"Well, since you asked. I—you know—I've been gone a long time, and don't know many people in Serendipity anymore. Mother is doing well, and doesn't need me around 24/7. In fact, she likes to have space to herself, and is too nice to say I'm crowding her. I wondered, if you have some time, maybe you and I could...just...hang out. If it's convenient."

Wow, was that the most garbled speech ever made? I was pretty sure it ranked in my personal top ten percent for rambling half-truths, too.

His eyes narrowed as he sized up what I'd said. "Sure thing. Tuesday's a day off for me, if you think Reba will need a non-crowded hour or two."

My mental list said I was going to wash

windows inside and out on the main floor, and find a handyman to do the outside of the second story windows. It was a tradition with our family—windows should be sparkling clean before winter set in, when you were stuck inside much of the time due to the weather. But officially Mother and I had nothing planned, unless she had an idea for an outing that I was unaware of.

"Tuesday seems like a possibility. I'll check with Mother, and call you. Okay?"

His eyes sparkled with humor now, as he enjoyed my discomfort. Did he think I was coming on to him? Yikes—that would set the wrong tone, but how to avoid it? I mean, man and woman, former teenage *item*, separated all these years, and now tossed together by the vagaries of life. It sounded like a partial plot for a romance novel, didn't it? But I didn't want Nick to get the wrong idea, and make our *relationship* even more complicated than it was.

He tipped his head in assent. "That works. I need to get to the clerk's office now, okay? Later."

He was up the steps and inside the heavy door,

taking the creeping cold sensation with him. I stood there processing the fact that I had just been sort of snubbed. Nick hadn't given me time to point out that if we did spend a couple of hours together, it had to be strictly platonic. His behavior suggested he had nothing else in mind.

That irritated me. I was trying to do the guy a favor, after all. The signs pointed very strongly to the fact that he needed the gift I had. So many years, and he hadn't managed to get his life and his soul in order, but I came along and was going to change that, so he could walk into his future whole and happy.

The least he could do was try to get me interested in a romantic interlude. Then I could have the satisfaction of turning him down. Not because I wanted to, as I was edging toward admitting that a non-platonic relationship with Nick Marshall sounded terrific. But it couldn't happen—I couldn't let it—due to my gift. This was one of the many times that it felt like more of a curse.

I wondered, again, why Grandma hadn't felt that way about it. Needing some encouragement, I went back to the pharmacy, bellied up to the soda fountain, and ordered two large chocolate malts to go. Mother loved malts, and could use an extra pound or two, having lost a bit of weight since her accident. If she was lucky, I wouldn't have drunk them both by the time I walked back up the hill to her house.

Chapter Eight

WHEN I GOT to Mother's, she was thrilled about the malt, accepted the bag of medicine, the cash, and her tax receipt, and told me in a no-nonsense voice to call my sister.

"Jennifer has been wanting some time with you, Jacqueline. You shouldn't keep to yourself so much. You know I'm doing fine." She softened the rejoinder with a sweet smile.

My sister and I have never been close. Due to our age difference of almost ten years, I was more of an albatross than a friend to her when she lived at our parents' home. When I finished high school, Jen was married to Marcus, and months away from sending Emily to kindergarten. I left that summer, and we never had an easy opportunity to connect as adults. I had given up expecting it.

She answered her cell right away. "Hi, Jacquie. Mother told you what I want?"

"She said I should call. That's all I know. Why? Is something up?"

"No, not really. I just wondered if you and I could do something together. Lillian came home from her trip today, and she's planning to spend most of tomorrow with Mother. I can get someone to cover the store. If you're free, I mean. And if you want to. "

"Want to do what, Jen?" That sounded harsh, but the words had tumbled out. "If you have something particular in mind. But sure, I'd love to hang out with you. Sounds good."

Jen put her hand over the phone mouthpiece and said something to—I assumed Marcus. Then, "Great. I'll pick you up around ten, and we'll play it by ear."

That was all we could do, I thought, as I went back into the kitchen where Mother was enjoying her drink. It wasn't as if Jen and I could re-create memories, visit our old haunts. Because she and I didn't share things like that. I acted happy about it to Mother, and helped her anticipate her day with Lillian. What would it be like to have a best friend for more decades than your children had been alive? I'd never know. The way my life was going, I'd never know what it was like to have a friend for more than a few weeks.

The feeling of being old and worn out washed over me. Being in Serendipity, where relationships lasted forever, made me realize how much I was missing by always being on the road. But I didn't see the old hometown through unrealistic rosy glass. Enough people remembered my past here, and wouldn't let go of it. That meant no rest for the weary—not in Serendipity, anyway.

****

Jen and I left shortly after ten, after we'd both gotten the requisite hugs from Lillian, who pulled into the drive a few minutes earlier. You'd have thought Lillian and I were close, the way she accepted me. Being my mother's daughter was good enough for her, I guessed. I didn't remember Lillian well from my youth, having paid as little attention to my elders as possible, like many kids. But now I recognized her strength of character and kindness. No wonder she and Mother were so tight.

Jen backed her van out of the drive. "Where to? The world is our oyster, as long as we can get back a little before four."

That's when Lillian was committed to be at the hospital, to pull part of someone's shift in the gift shop.

"I don't care, Jen. Whatever you want to do, really. Anything we see will be new to me."

"Not unless we get out of the county." She shifted into drive and headed north on Shelby, toward the highway. "And that's a great idea. Less chance of getting interrupted, running into people we know."

"People *you* know."

She turned left and we headed out of town. "Okay. Whatever. Bloomington work for you?"

I watched the houses and small businesses glide past my side window. "Sure. I haven't been up there in forever. There's always lots to see."

"You won't believe how built-up it is along 37."

All I could picture was a straight highway going north and south. "I don't remember what it looked like *then*. IU is your alma mater, not mine." Maybe I had dreamed of an Indiana University degree, but lots of dreams got left in the dirt.

"Sure, I know. I just thought you might notice the change compared to times the family drove up to see me."

"Right. Maybe I will." But I doubted it. I'd been wrapped up in my own life back then. Not so different from now, perhaps. I cleared my throat, hesitant to bring up my concern. "The only thing is...so many people."

She took a quick breath. "Sorry—I wasn't thinking." She turned up the hill to follow Highway 60. "How about Spring Mill? We can stroll around the village, get a nice lunch at the inn. If there's a bus load of school kids, we'll head out on a hiking trail."

I did remember the state park. It was a beautiful reserve of old-growth forest, with a reconstructed pioneer village, and a beautiful inn. Plenty of acreage, not a crush of people. "That sounds ideal, Jen. Thanks for suggesting it."

The trip took a little more than half an hour, and with just that much change in latitude, the lavish increase in fall color was amazing.

She parked in a nearly-empty lot, and we grabbed our jackets and started a slow stroll along the path, past play areas and picnic tables. The briskly flowing spring that fed the old mill added its music to songs the birds were singing in the huge trees whose leaves were bright yellow and red, interspersed with some green hold-outs. The place was the epitome of peace, but I remembered school trips here. The peace could quickly turn to excited mayhem. But for now it was perfect. I filled my lungs with the fresh, cool air.

"I've enjoyed the hints of fall around Serendipity. This is a nice forecast of what's coming."

"Just a few miles north makes a difference," she said, looking around as if the scenery was new to her. "It's so beautiful, isn't it? I never get tired of the seasons. I love all four of them. Can't imagine living in a different climate, not getting to see the changes."

I picked up a large, brown leaf, and twirled it by

the stem as we walked. "Lots of people love the beach, the high mountains, or the desert. Each has its unique type of beauty."

I'd spent plenty of time in all of them, and more. "But I agree, this area in the fall is awesome. Since Indiana is a fly-over state, the natural beauty is sort of a well-kept secret. Back in the day, there wasn't much to bring people here. To the state, and especially to Serendipity. What about now? I'm not seeing a lot of new industry around town."

She shook her head. "Not much is new, but Carla's husband Jared is the director of economic development now. He has good ideas. We've got a very long way to go if we're ever going to change the movement of all the kids who leave to find careers, and never come back to live."

This was a long-standing problem. Mother had talked about her concerns that Jen and Marcus's kids would never come back to Serendipity. "It's great that Emily decided to stay. But I guess the twins and Ben won't find jobs anywhere near?"

She stopped, watching a couple of squirrels

chase each other around the trunk of a tree. "West coast is more likely. I don't like the idea, but there it is. And if you recall, Emily didn't finish college. Kids without a career in mind are more likely to stay around, maybe hoping for a factory job to open up."

Marcus was in management at a local factory, but most of the other big employers had moved operations overseas.

"Yes, I do remember Emily had...a rough patch."

Jen started walking again. "Ha. Her rough patch lasted about ten years. That girl took every wrong turn she came to."

"Until her car wreck." The words came out in a rush, and I couldn't call them back. I touched Jen's shoulder, hoping to soften their effect.

She looked at me, her eyes bright with sudden, unshed tears. "Yes. The wreck that almost killed her, ended up saving her life. It's a huge blessing to have my daughter back again."

"I'm so glad for everyone, Jen. And that little Isabel—what a beauty she is."

She stopped at a Y in the path, indicating I should choose the direction. I led the way to the left, in front of a cabin that was backed up against a steep, tree-covered hill.

Jen continued. "I almost feel sorry for Emily sometimes. She put our family through a lot, and I imagine Isabel will do the same to her. You love them so much, Jacquie, that when they make mistakes, it hurts you as much or more than it does them. But you can't make their decisions for them, once they get past a certain age."

"Are we still talking about Emily, or have we moved to the subject of my history, and how it has affected Mother? And you?" Mother, sure. But Jen's life was so separate from mine, we could have been cousins instead of sisters.

She stopped again, in the middle of the path, and faced me. "Guess I'm pretty transparent."

"Yep. So, what do you suggest I do? Is it harder for Mother that I'm here, but will be gone soon? Should I have stayed away and let you deal with the situation in your ever-capable manner?" I held up both hands.

"Don't get me wrong. I mean that. Everyone knows you're the reliable daughter. I'm the bad seed."

"Don't say that. You're not bad. You're just...different."

She was being kind, for some reason. "Wouldn't you say it's the same thing, in the minds of most people in our hometown?"

"So? Since when do you care so much about what people think? You weren't like that as a kid."

"What was I like? You have no idea. You weren't around much when I was growing up, you know. You never had time for me."

"You have a selective memory. I was around plenty, Jacquie. I saw you change from a normal, active kid with a group of friends, to someone who was frightened and self-conscious."

"You'd have been self-conscious too, if you'd been saddled with a gift that destroyed your life. But no, you got to be normal, on top of being the good girl."

Jen's eyes flashed. "Jacqueline Markland, listen to yourself. Don't you remember what Grandma said to you about the gift? That day we were at their house, and

Marcus and Jamison stopped by?"

I leveled a severe look at her. "Sure, I remember. But she said it just to *me*. You weren't there."

Her cheeks turned pink. "I was in the house, and I managed to hover outside the door part of the time. Man, Jacquie, I was so jealous. I was the older one, yet you got Grandma's gift. What a rip-off."

"Seriously? I'd love to hand it over to you. Be glad to do that right now, except it's impossible."

She sighed. "It was so unfair. I just did normal stuff like finish college, get married, and have kids. Wait—that sounds horrible. I love Marcus and the kids. I love *my life*. But it's awfully tame compared to yours."

"You're jealous of me living in a van?"

"It's the cutest little RV I've ever seen, and doesn't look like an RV. You're out traveling all over the country, and taking trips to Europe, writing beautiful articles for the travel companies. You really found your niche, writing about sleepy towns off the beaten track. I subscribe to travel magazines and follow blogs just so I can read what you write. I'll never see those places in person."

"You could. You and Marcus—"

She shook her head. "Marcus and I are lucky to get two weeks' vacation. Half of that is spent working on whatever part of the house needs attention each year. No, we've invested our time and money in our family and our home, and there are no regrets. But—I thought you realized how much I admire what you do."

What she omitted was the long weekend each year that she, Marcus, and their kids spent with me, and Mother. I hadn't thought about the hardship that created for them.

The autumn scenery blurred, and the lumbering sound of the grist mill's huge, wooden water wheel faded, as I attempted to process what she'd said. My sister was envious of what I had, when my wish was to be a normal person like her.

Jen put her arm around my shoulders, pulling me along the path and back into the moment. "So, what are you going to do about Nick?"

"I—what do you mean?" Did Jen realize the

sensations he was giving off? Maybe she had some of the gift after all.

"Don't play innocent. You and he had a thing going, and it doesn't take a clairvoyant to detect the undercurrents between you."

"Jen, again I have to point out you haven't been in on a discussion." The one with Grandma that she had eavesdropped on, I had no trouble believing, but she hadn't been in the same building with Nick and me at all since I got here.

"I saw the two of you talking on the courthouse steps. I was at the shop, remember? Those two ladies finally left, I walked them out, and when I looked across the street, you and Nick were having this body language discussion. I could almost see the sparks fly."

"You are kidding me. You've made an assumption about Nick and me being attracted to each other, based on a glance at the two of us, fifty yards away?" Oh, the small town mentality!

"Sweetheart, it wasn't a glance. I saw him get out of his police cruiser, notice you, pause a couple of minutes until you and Carla finished talking, and she started up the steps. I saw the way he watches you when you talk."

Part of me wanted to believe Nick was interested, but the rest of me knew that was a dead-end. "Jen, seriously, you need to get a life."

She laughed. "I have one, and it's in a small town where we watch out for each other."

"You mean spy on each other. That's kinda creepy."

"Put your own spin on the truth if you will. I'm just saying, here you both are, back in Serendipity, and in the very same houses where you were when things fell apart. Seems like that's almost like an omen. At the very least, you've got a second chance with him. I ask again: What are you going to do about Nick?"

We had wandered under the stone arch, into the garden area. The flowers were done for the year, and fallen leaves had blown into the dying foliage. I sat on a bench, and she joined me.

"There's nothing I *can* do. Sure, he still sets my pulse racing—"

"I knew it!"

"But there's no future in a relationship between the two of us. I'm not going to stay in Serendipity. He's put down some deep roots, by the look of it."

I didn't want to tell her about the need I felt from Nick, or the fact that I was perplexed to figure out what it was, and how to help him overcome it.

"Tell me why you can't stay. Is it *can't*, or *won't*?"

"You know I can't. Everybody remembers my history. Plus I can't let people get too close and maybe figure out the truth about my gift. You know anything out of the ordinary is distrusted, or worse. I don't feel like dealing with that, and putting Mother in that spotlight is unthinkable."

"Mother created a new life for herself after Dad died. She helped my Emily find her own future. And she fell down a flight of stairs, landed on thinly-padded concrete, and broke one tiny bone. She is *not* that delicate, Jacquie." She took a deep breath, and when she spoke again her voice was calmer. "Did you ever think how much she misses you? That having you here would be better for her?"

"I miss her, too. And you, and I've missed all the milestones of your kids' lives."

"Then stay, Jacquie. Put your fears aside, and stay in Serendipity. Mother and I are in your corner. So is Marcus, and Emily. Heck, the whole Standish family comes along with the deal. Matthew has already given you the thumbs-up, according to Emily. How bad can it be, to face those moments of your past that you're not proud of? We've all made mistakes."

"I'll think about it, okay? No promises. And just to clarify, I'm considering your request that I stay because of my family. Not because of Nick Marshall."

And I meant that, mostly.

Chapter Nine

THE DAY WITH Jennifer had given me a new way to look at my life. That she thought I could overcome my history in Serendipity, settle here, and have a happy existence was laughable. It surprised me that I wasn't laughing.

Since I arrived, the little town's charms had been working on me, getting me to relax more, making me feel at home. But I'd been insulated from the gossip tree. Maybe, as Jen said, Mother was tough enough to take the garbage it could throw. Perhaps having me nearby instead of always on the run would make it worthwhile to her.

I didn't want to discuss any possibilities with Mother—yet. I had to mull them over, try to picture a future here. I wouldn't want to get her hopes up, only to stomp on them later. For instance, a travel writer didn't stay in the same small town twelve months of the year. What job could I find in Serendipity, or within reasonable commuting distance, that could support even my modest lifestyle? Would my gift become apparent to the town folk? And if so, what kind of outcry would be raised?

I didn't belong here. Didn't belong anywhere.

Jen's insistent question kept up a sing-song in my ear. *So, what are you going to do about Nick?* Not for the reason she had in mind, I did need to figure out the answer to that question. I looked forward to Tuesday. Maybe everything would become clear to me when he and I spent extended time together. Once his problem was dealt with, I could focus on my own possibilities.

I had gleaned a little bit of information from Jen about Stacy, the bank teller. Her husband had left her for someone he'd met online. The guy had moved to Canada, was paying zero child support, and didn't have the decency to keep in touch with his teenage daughter.

I felt terrible for Stacy and the girl, but felt a strong pull to finish up with Nick before I tried to get close to Stacy, and help her.

****

As set up in a couple of short, businesslike texts, Nick arrived at Mother's front door promptly at eight on Tuesday morning. Not an early riser by choice, I'd barely managed to perform my morning rituals and dress in jeans and a sweater by the time the doorbell rang. I was sticking my feet into a pair of loafers when I heard her open the door and exclaim how happy she was to see her favorite next-door neighbor. Not such huge praise, since she lives on a corner and only has one neighbor next-door. I wondered if he realized she might not be his biggest fan, then calmed down my angry morning self with the truth. Mother adored Nick. Always had, always would. She liked his honesty, his goodness, and his sense of humor. I grabbed a jacket off the bedpost and hitched my cross-body bag over my head. The two of them were on the sofa, laughing like loons over a stupid joke he had told.

"Seriously. Is this much comedy appropriate for such an early hour?"

Mother nudged Nick. "Don't mind Jacqueline. She never has been a morning person." Looking at me, she tipped her head. "Have you had your sixteen ounces of coffee, dear?"

"No. I was rushed."

"Well, I'm sure you have time to get a to-go cup. Whatever it takes to replace that sour face with your beautiful smile."

Nick nodded. "If you want, we can grab a late breakfast in Mendacious. I know a little place. Not too packed with people this time of morning, excellent coffee." Nick waggled his eyebrows in encouragement.

I'd need plenty of coffee to be alert to what I was *supposed* to be doing with Nick. "Okay. That sounds good." I gave Mother a hug and kiss. "You be sure to call Jen if you need her, right? Or Lillian?"

She nodded. "Or Emily, her sisters-in-law Francie, Carla, Melissa, or anyone else on that long list we made."

"And you have your cell?"

She pulled it out of her pocket. "Yes, and it's charged, and the aforesaid numbers programmed into it. Go. Have fun. Relax."

Nick laughed as Mother made a shooing motion with both hands. He opened the door for me and we headed out on our day of discovery. First, excellent coffee in Mendacious, then the truth about what Nick needed, in order to be whole.

The drive to Mendacious was okay. We listened to a public radio station out of Louisville that played an eclectic mix. The creeping cold up and down my spine, that had started the moment I saw Nick in the living room, didn't stop. Watching his relaxed profile as he drove continued to perplex me. How could he be in such strong need and not show even one outward sign?

Maybe I could get him to spill some information if I got him talking about himself. I felt awkward asking questions, because I had more than one motivation. The one I was supposed to have, plus the personal desire— stronger each time I saw him—that he and I could find a way to be together. I knew it was impossible, but that didn't keep me from wanting it. I would do some gently inquiry. The worst he could do was tell me to mind my own business.

"Umm. I remember you said, that night when you cooked the steaks?" I cleared my throat, hoping to form normal sentences. "I remember you said something happened where you were living, that made you ready to relocate to Serendipity when you inherited your aunt and uncle's house. I don't think you mentioned where you were, or what you were doing. Have you always been a police officer? You went to Duke, right? I thought you were interested in an engineering degree. Did you change your major?" I screeched to a halt, appalled that my questions had tumbled over each other like autumn leaves caught in a whirlwind.

Brandi Carlile's voice filled the car, and I wondered if Nick was going to speak at all.

"Which question do you want me to answer first? I've had the feeling you didn't want to be around me, weren't interested in anything about me. So forgive my surprise at the barrage of inquiries."

"You don't have to act superior, Nick. If you

don't want to answer, that's fine." The cold sensation crept over my scalp.

"I'm not acting superior." He sighed. "Okay, I could have worded that differently. Let me give you the short version. I went to Duke, intending to get that engineering degree. But it didn't happen. I didn't study as hard as I should have, my grades suffered, and my parents refused any more money. I was working and paying part of expenses, and I had a scholarship, but without my parents' support, I couldn't make it. I went back to Chicago, to live with them and try to figure out what to do next. My parents were out one night, going to a concert downtown, and were killed in a hit-and-run."

My heart lurched at the picture. "Oh, Nick! I'm so sorry. I had no idea." Why hadn't Mother told me?

He sent me a quick, pained glance. "I know. You were long gone."

He ran a hand through his hair. "I was at the police station every day, asking if they'd gotten any clues. Those officers had to be sick to death of me, but they never brushed me off. After a year or so, I'd lost both of my part-time jobs because I didn't care about anything but finding the guy who'd done that, and gotten away with it."

"Did they find him? Or her?"

"No. Never did. But I'd spent so much time at the station, and got interested in the day-to-day work. Trying to uphold the law, protect people, seeing that justice is served. Some of the guys suggested I try to get into the police academy." A brief smile flashed across his face. "And the rest is history."

"But not." That didn't explain him working in Serendipity.

"Yeah, you're right. I got out on a beat, was doing okay. But everything about the city was a reminder of my parents, you know? It hurt more and more, and one day I was called to the scene of a hit-and-run. That was it; I was ready to leave. I care about the work. Sometimes more than might be healthy. But I just couldn't do it in Chicago anymore."

"Wasn't long after that, I got the call about Uncle Ed dying. We'd lost Aunt Georgia a few months earlier. I made the trip down for his service. They'd planned it all ahead of time, so the far-flung cousins and I didn't have to make any decisions, just show up. When it was over, the lawyer took me aside and told me about the house. In a way, it was an answer to a prayer I'd never prayed. I told the guy—well, you know him. The lawyer is Jim Standish. Anyway, I told Jim I couldn't move here without a job, and he said there was an opening at the local PD. How weird is that? They didn't have any candidates with experience, so I basically walked in and was hired. Luckiest break I ever got."

A few beats on the radio passed when neither of us spoke.

"Nick, I feel horrible that I didn't know about your parents. I wonder why Mother and Jen never told me."

"What difference would it have made? You couldn't have done anything about it."

No? Maybe I could have. What about being there for him, so he didn't have to face those months alone when he was trying to find out the truth, becoming so despondent that he'd lost his jobs? What about using my gift to help him become whole again?

I shot him a look. His face was back to normal. Handsome, relaxed. So he was putting up a good front, but now I knew about his loss. How to fill the void his parents' death had left, though? That was the challenge. I could do it. Had to do it. Because of my personal feelings for Nick, I was even more resolved than usual to make certain I did my very best with the task at hand.

"It's great that you're settled here, and making a good life. I'm sure the town appreciates the work you do."

"They seem to," he said. "One thing about Serendipity, whatever you do, good or bad, there's a major ripple effect. Not like in a big city. Around here, with everybody either related to each other, or being a friend, neighbor, or co-worker, the connections just never end."

How well I knew the truth of those words. Except, unlike Nick, the ripples I'd made had been bad.

Chapter Ten

AS FAR BACK into my childhood as I can remember, Nick Marshall spent a month each summer with his aunt and uncle next door to us. The weeks he lived at Ed and Georgia's were brighter than the rest of the year. Most of the neighborhood at that time was couples whose kids were raised and had gone somewhere else to earn a living. My girlfriends from school lived far enough away that we didn't see each other as often as we wanted, during school breaks.

My high school years, as my gift grew stronger, were disastrous. I wanted to keep from having the sensations, and dealing with everyone's problems. The only thing I could think of was to cut myself off from people. If I wasn't around anyone, their needs couldn't trigger the gift. I withdrew from extracurricular activities I had previously enjoyed. I even dropped out of the church youth group, to my parents' deep regret. And I skipped school dozens of times. I became a different person, in an attempt at self-preservation.

When I was at school, I ended up in the principal's and school counselor's office more times than I could count. If I wasn't there for truancy, it was insubordination. I refused to dress for gym class, because the crush of girls in the locker room made me feel as if I might explode. I insisted on sitting in the last row of every classroom, closest to the door. Field trips? I had loved them before my world changed so drastically, but as the gift became stronger, riding a school bus full of classmates was unbearable. As time progressed, that became less of an issue, because my behavior problems resulted in me being banned from field trips.

The first time I tried alcohol, I had a fuzzy revelation that, although the respite would be temporary, it was better than none at all. I found ways to acquire a bottle when I needed one. When forced to be around people, I compensated by drinking afterward, trying to forget the sensations their needs evoked.

My parents were at a loss of how to help me, I was a giant embarrassment to my sister, friends I'd had since elementary school fell away one by one. Because of grades that had gone from honor roll to toilet bowl, I barely managed to graduate, and we all knew I couldn't hack college.

And the Gossip Tree hung me high. In four years I'd gone from being the quiet younger daughter, to a troublemaker whose every step was questioned. In the background the whispers were along the lines of, "That Jacqueline Markland is such a disappointment. Poor Reba and Geoffrey didn't raise her to be a juvenile delinquent."

Never mind that my parents and I had a good, solid relationship. We loved each other unconditionally, but without Grandma's direction, I was too immature to handle the gift that presided over my life.

High school is when Nick and I fell apart—I found ways to avoid him. It was torture to stay away, but I had to. In spite of wanting to be more than summertime friends with Nick, it was impossible.

Because he was outgoing and athletic, he made new friends in town. Some of the SHS boys drafted him onto a summer baseball league, and even though he only played one month each year with the little team, he was a star.

The summer after high school, Nick spent his month at Ed and Georgia's, said good-bye and returned to his parents' home in Chicago. Next stop: Duke University, and after that I'd never see him again. We had both known for years that this day was coming. As we matured, and I became reclusive, Nick's outgoing nature became more prominent. He loved being in groups, going to concerts and sporting events. He had everything going for him—good looks, social ease, and a career path that would ensure financial success. Why had I ever thought he could care for me?

That last day, he spoke to me quietly, beneath the ancient oak tree in the side yard, as his aunt and uncle fussed to make sure he had a lunch packed in the car, and all the stuff from his room in its trunk. He told me I needed to figure out my life, because if I didn't, I was going to *crash and burn*. I was the only one who could decide.

I was hurt by his lecture, because I'd fallen in love with Nick, and my gift made a future with him impossible. But Nick was angry. It came off him in waves so strong I leaned against the tree to keep my balance. After he climbed into his Corvette and drove away, I made it to my bedroom and closed the door before I started to cry.

But I didn't cry for long. Nick's departure strengthened my resolve to find a different way to live. It was bad enough for my parents now, but if the simple folks here knew the truth about me, disaster would strike. I knew nobody would believe or understand the reality, so the obvious reaction would be contempt.

I needed a new start, and the way to get it was to leave Serendipity forever. To protect the people I loved, I needed to stay away from them.

I found as much peace as I could through my vagabond life, though that was a constant challenge. Being back in Serendipity these last few weeks had been more enjoyable than I'd expected, except for

Nick's presence on the scene, and now my niggling worry about Stacy.

I'd never imagined having Nick as a next-door neighbor again, even temporarily. I was trying hard not to send him any signals that revealed what was going on inside me. It was the worst news ever—after all these years, I was still in love with him.

****

As promised, breakfast was delicious, and the restaurant was sparsely occupied.

"I remember you never liked crowds," Nick said when he noticed me sitting up straighter as the door opened and a noisy group of four entered. "You never told me why, of course."

"Just don't like them. Give me wide open spaces every time." I kept my voice light, hoping he wouldn't press the issue.

"Jacqueline Markland, the girl who hates crowds and won't share her burdens with people who care enough to help." His eyebrows rose. "We're all grown up now, Jacquie. I'm not angry anymore about you not coming to watch me play baseball."

This isn't about me, Mister. I don't want to think about those memories.

I couldn't let him get me riled, though. It would only slow me down on what I needed to be doing for him. I forced out a laugh about our old fight. "I'm glad to hear you're okay now, Nick. You shouldn't have been angry about it back then."

"More hurt than angry, but I had my pride. I wanted to show off for you. Did you realize that?"

"No. Well, maybe. You were sure mad enough when you didn't see me at the game. I remember the look on your face when you pounded on our front door that afternoon."

He went on as if I hadn't spoken. "I was a decent player, you know. It gave me a way to make new friends."

"Since I was worthless as a friend."

"Not worthless! But I couldn't count on you, Jacquie. One minute you'd be fine, and the next, you didn't want to do anything fun."

"I didn't want to go out with a group of noisy

people. It's not the same thing."

"Seemed like it." His features were set. He didn't believe I had good reasons for my choices.

"Well, you're wrong, Nick. I enjoy getting out and seeing new places, having new experiences, but it becomes miserable for me—not fun—in a crowd."

He leaned back, his arms crossed.

"Why?" It was a dare.

I could tell him some things, but not everything because he'd never comprehend it. Answering at all was taking a chance, but maybe if I won his confidence he would open up to me, and my job would be easier.

I held the coffee cup between both hands on the table, needing its warmth. "It's hard to explain. In a crowd, I become very affected by the emotions of the people around me. If you don't have that experience, I don't think you'll understand. It's almost as if the strength of their anger, hurt, even excitement becomes a drain on my strength. Put me in an angry crowd, and once I manage to get back to my van, I'm likely to be in bed for days."

I shrugged as if it wasn't a big deal. "Does that

make any sense to you?"

He'd been listening, and seemed to be deciding whether I was being honest. "It makes a kind of sense, I suppose. At least it coordinates with what I remember. Have you tried to find out why you have this overreaction to others' emotions?"

"Believe me, I've done what I can. The only answer is to avoid crowds, notice signs that I'm having trouble, and rest when I need to." I took a breath, then decided to tell him more. "And for what it's worth, I did go to your ballgame. The tourney game, that summer your team won. I made myself go, because it was so important to you."

My palms got clammy, as I recalled the day. "I didn't climb into the grandstand, but stood a little distance away, hoping I'd be all right. But it was awful. The screaming and cursing."

"Oh? The team? I don't remember that."

"No, not the team. The parents. They were yelling at the officials, at the coach, and at each other's kids. I didn't last there very long. I wish you'd looked over and seen me. At least you'd know I'm telling the truth now."

"I don't doubt you were there, Jacquie. I've never known you to lie." His voice was soft, and his eyes kind. "The obvious question is, *why didn't you tell me this before?*"

"I couldn't risk being different. You know Serendipity doesn't exactly embrace diversity."

"But you *were* different, and still are. Why not just let people get used to that, instead of putting yourself through all the self-defeating behaviors?"

"I had my reasons. Besides, that's ancient history."

"No, you're doing the same thing now. You're showing a face to the public that isn't who you really are. It's okay to be yourself, Jacquie, even in Serendipity. You might be surprised how well accepted you'd be."

I sipped the coffee that didn't taste so great anymore. I wanted to believe what he said, but knew it was false. *Me, fit in?*

He smiled sadly. "The town has been good to me. Gave me a second chance when I needed it, and the community has kind of become my family. I'm not sure what'll happen if I leave."

"*Leave?* You're just telling me how great it is, and you're getting ready to leave?" This was some déjà vu I could do without.

Not meeting my eyes, he moved eggs around his plate with his fork. "Maybe you remember, Dad was pushing me to get an engineering degree. At Duke. Like he had done."

"When all your life, you'd wanted to be a police officer." How many dozen times had he told me that?

"I failed him. Even now, I wonder if I should try to go back to school, give it another shot. My heart isn't there, though. It's here, and in the work I do. I think I'm where I'm supposed to be..."

"If that's what you feel, deep down, then it's true."

"Maybe. Still, sometimes I have doubts." He looked deep into my eyes, deciding whether to share more. "I've got a chance to be chief. The current chief is retiring at the end of the year. I have to let the mayor know soon, whether or not I'll take the appointment."

Maybe we were getting to the meat of the matter now. "What's making you hesitate? Afraid of the additional hours and responsibility?"

"No, nothing like that. I just want to be one hundred percent sure before I say *yes*. I never want to do something halfheartedly, like I did in college. My dad never completely forgave me. He tried to, but didn't quite get there."

"And you haven't forgiven yourself."

He shrugged. "Probably not, but I'm working on it. I know he wanted the best for me, and he just didn't realize that being like him wasn't the answer."

When Nick left for college, I thought he had everything going for him. His life was mapped out, he was handsome, smart, and loved being with people. But underneath all that was a boy who had just graduated high school and was headed away from the career he'd always wanted. No amount of financial or other success would have made up for that loss. That day under the oak tree before he left, I'd felt waves of anger from him. Some of it was directed at me because he knew I was messing up my life. But now I realized some of the anger was at his father, or even at himself for not standing up to his parents.

Without realizing I was going to do it, I put my hand over his, on the table. He turned his palm up and curled his fingers around mine. The cold inside me was a piercing pain, but I managed a smile. "Maybe you and I have more in common than I realized, Nick. We've been living our lives with some hurtful secrets."

Thank goodness for the waitress who dropped a pot of coffee on the floor, creating a terrible mess, and a general uproar. It broke not only the glass carafe, but the mood in which I'd been tempted to tell him the whole truth about me.

We went to the forestry a few miles from Mendacious, hiked a couple of trails in near-silence, and climbed the fire tower for a gorgeous view. I knew Nick wouldn't let the matter die, and I wasn't sure how long I could side-step his questioning. Did I even want to? Keeping my secret when I traveled from town to town wasn't difficult. Over time, I learned how to be an interested listener without seeming creepy, when I became aware of someone who needed my help. But being back in Serendipity it was different. *I* was different, especially with Nick.

"Thanks for bringing me here," I was breathing hard from the exertion of the climb as I walked to all sides of the tower, to take in as much of the beauty as I could.

"It's one of my favorite places. The whole forestry is, but especially the tower, and in October. The color has nearly peaked. I know the hordes descend on Brown County this time of year, but I like the view I've got." He paused, stepped back. "And the current view is the best ever."

I dragged my eyes from the magnificent variety of color that stretched to the horizon. When I looked at Nick, he was focused entirely on me.

He reached out, gently ran his fingers through my hair, and touched my cheek. My breath caught.

"Autumn is your season, Jacquie. Your silky, flaming hair, your sparkling green eyes flecked with gold. You're so full of life, but then...you disappear." He dropped his hand away, and gestured to the vista all around us. "Just like the leaves, in this brief, glorious display. How have I seen so many autumns without realizing you're the embodiment of my favorite time of year? Or, maybe autumn has been my favorite because it reminded me of you."

God help me, I felt like crying. Was he going to kiss me? I wanted him to—desperately wanted it—but wasn't sure what effect that would have on the task I was supposed to be doing for him. That had to be paramount.

Didn't it?

"Do you have to disappear this time, Jacquie? Or can you stay, and tell me your secrets?"

He knew I hadn't been completely truthful. I wanted to tell him, but knew I shouldn't. "You're better off not knowing, Nick."

He took my hand. "I disagree. All these years I've wondered, you know. Why you pushed me away, faded into the shadows, and wouldn't let me close. I wanted to be close to you, Jacquie." He laughed. "Raging hormones aside, we had been great friends, at least one month of the year. I thought we had something special."

This wasn't helping my pulse-rate return to normal. The truth could only lead to misunderstanding, or treatment as a freak. I'd suffered enough of that in the past. I couldn't survive receiving it from Nick.

A long moment passed, and we heard a group clambering up the stairway.

Nick's shoulders sagged, and his smile was sad. "I didn't really expect an answer. Not the one I wanted, anyway." He jerked a thumb toward the stairs. "We'd better start down. There's a place halfway that's wide enough to meet and pass people."

That was the end of the almost-kiss. The end of another awkward moment in which I wasn't sure where my loyalties would fall. If Nick had continued in that vein, I might have tried to follow. Forget repairing his soul, and move on to making a life with him.

Ridiculous thoughts. I should be glad for the noisy family we met on the stairs, and glad for the call from the dispatcher saying one of the officers had flu and needed to go home; could Nick come in?

So we returned to Serendipity right away. I should be glad. I told him I could easily walk to

Mother's from the police station. It was just a few blocks.

His smile was quick. "I have to change into my uniform and take the cruiser instead of my own vehicle. But thanks."

Mother had left a note on the kitchen table. She was at Lillian's, getting ready for the Halloween event. I should call when I got home.

But I sank onto the couch for a few minutes, comforted by Sam's purring presence.

"So close, Sam. Nick and I—we've still got a wedge between us, and I'm not sure what it is. Once that's gone, though...."

Sam walked over my legs purring and tickling my nose with his tail.

I pushed his tail away, pulled him in to cuddle, as I re-lived the too-short time I'd had with Nick. I enjoyed myself and he seemed to, as well.

I leaned down and spoke into Sam's ear. "I'm not dragging my feet, you know. I really am trying to learn what it was his soul lacks." Nick's concern for others was one of the things I'd always loved about him. It made him good at his job, I assumed, as long as he was able to avoid being overwhelmed by the enormity of his responsibility.

On a personal level, I felt calm and comfortable with him, despite the cold, creeping awareness that was present whenever I was around him. I was accustomed to the awareness—it was to me what a time clock is to someone who works in a store or factory.

Cold, creeping awareness. Time to do your work.

Nick made me laugh, when recalling silly antics of our childhood summers. He made me cry, relating some of the things that happened in our community. Kids or senior citizens who were neglected, or worse. The growing drug problem that nobody could get a handle on. And other maladies that related in one way or another, to the county's severely limited employment opportunities.

I wished our day had been longer, and regretted the fact that, as he mentioned, I'd soon be gone, like the autumn colors. Once Mother was up to speed, and Nick's soul was repaired, there was no reason to stay.

Chapter Eleven

NICK CAME OVER a few days later, bringing Mother a pumpkin pie he'd bought at a bake sale.

"Talk to you outside, Jacquie?" he asked quietly when he was about to leave.

Mother smiled, pretending she hadn't heard, and went into the kitchen with the pie.

Once we were outside on the glider, he invited me to participate with him in Trunk or Treat at the Christmas tree farm.

"I thought I'd do something different this year, if you're up to a challenge. If we used your van for the loot, we could decorate it like a Gypsy wagon, and both of us could be Gypsies. What do you think? I usually dress like an Old West sheriff, but this year...not sure why…I just had this idea." He looked across at me, seated so close that I was intoxicated by his unmistakable manly scent, as well as his boyish excitement about Halloween.

I squeezed my eyes shut, reminding myself not to let our relationship get too personal. And of all things, I didn't want to be in the middle of the Halloween hoopla, surrounded by kids and parents who might or might not set off my gift.

"You know about me and crowds. I'm not sure I'd be much fun." *Or be able to handle the emotional roller-coaster without spending a couple of days in bed, recovering from it.*

"I've thought about that. Your van has tinted windows, and if you start to feel overwhelmed you could go inside it, let me deal with handing out the candy and stuff. Crowd thins, you come back out."

I had a set of noise-cancelling headphones that could help, too. It was a lot of effort for what might result in nothing, but Nick looked so hopeful, and I was running out of time to figure out his problem. Mother was fine now. I needed to hit the road soon.

"That *might* work," I said.

His smile grew wider. "I see the wheels turning. You're going to do it, aren't you?"

I laughed, unable to resist his enthusiasm. "Okay, you've talked me into it. I can manage a long skirt and blouse, some big hoop earrings." I was designing the outfit in my mind's eye. Just a little sewing with Mother's machine, and it could be really cute. A peasant blouse, off the shoulder... Wow. Maybe not a good idea. I was getting entirely too close to Nick. Emotionally, that is. Except for that brief hand-holding incident in the restaurant, and the time he'd touched my hair and cheek, we'd kept air between us. It was as if a force field separated us—there'd been times I knew he wanted to touch my face, lean down and kiss me, but he hadn't. Darn this gift. I'd lose Nick eventually—*again*—without ever having him at all.

Sam jumped into my lap and practically screamed into my face.

Nick reared back. "Geez! What's wrong with him?"

"I don't know." I picked up the cat and took him

into the house. He had food and water in the right location, and his litter pan was spotless. I tossed a bit of catnip onto the top of his cat condominium, and he scowled at me. *Scowled?*

Nick had come in behind me. "Looks like he's mad at you, huh? Not sure I've ever seen that look on a cat's face."

"He's fine. He'll be fine." Weird, weird cat. But I'd never known him to behave that way.

****

On Halloween night, everyone who'd signed up arrived early at the tree farm, where Jim and David Standish, Carla's husband Jared, and Francie's husband Brad, handed out maps and gave directions to the assigned spots sprinkled throughout the acreage.

We stopped at the Christmas shop, and walked in with Mother. Lillian swept her into a hug and the two started chattering about how much fun everyone would have tonight. Lillian offered us hot cider and popcorn balls, but we were in a hurry to get set up.

"Are you two ladies going to be okay here?" I

was concerned about leaving them to deal with a flood of people.

Smiling, Lillian waved my question away. "Francie is in charge of everything, so there's no telling where she is, but Melissa will be here to help in a while. Carla and Katie are doing something creative to Carla's Mustang. I hope to see pictures, because I think we'll be busy in here all evening. Oh! And Emily and Isabel will be joining us in the shop soon." She clapped her hands together, and beamed at Mother. "Isabel will be dressed as a darling pink lamb. Matthew and Miles have been swooping around in their superhero costumes for an hour or more. They're so cute—but don't tell them I used that word to describe them."

Satisfied that the ladies would be fine, I drove to the spot we'd been assigned. Everyone was working fiendishly to turn vehicles into something else entirely. The Van-Gypsy Wagon came out even better than I had expected. Nick had a talent at transformation I hadn't known about.

The tree farm's tiny-cabin bed and breakfast customers all decided to get in on the fun too, and the little buildings looked more cute than spooky with their orange pumpkin lights and fake bats swooping from the eaves.

For a Christmas tree farm, the place made a pretty terrific Halloween venue.

Nick's nearly jaw-dropping reaction made every minute of cutting and sewing the costume worthwhile. The white peasant blouse with long full sleeves left one shoulder bare. My skirt was vertical sections of bright silks and dark velvets, created from Mother's bag of retired clothes. I cinched it tight at the waist with a long gold sash. I wore my hair loose, but when I moved my head, the big hoop earrings still peeked out. I decided to go barefoot, and was relieved when the night was warmer than expected. Red nail polish on fingers and toes, and a heavy gold ankle bracelet completed the outfit.

Nick looked delicious as a Gypsy. He had created a mustache and goatee with some type of makeup, and had a heavy gold clip earring in one ear. The bandana on his head covered most of his dark hair, with just a few curls peeking out. Some hair showed in the deep V of his loose, silky shirt, too. Slim black jeans and black leather boots. *Mmm.* I wasn't the only woman appreciating his costume, and I paid special attention—professional reasons, of course—to Nick's reaction to each woman who stopped to chat with him. Not much reaction at all. I did notice, though, that he smiled at me a lot.

I don't know when it happened, exactly. It was sometime during the noisy fun of the Trunk or Treat, while Nick *oohed* and *aahed* over the cute or scary costume of each child, getting down on his haunches to look into the eyes of a tiny princess or ghost, handing out candy, receiving occasional hugs or sticky kisses on his cheek. Sometime that night I realized I had really messed up. Because I had fallen in love. And now, it wasn't just leftovers from the childish love I'd had for him years ago. This love was for real, though I knew it was doomed.

I couldn't get involved with a "client." My calling, my gift, was to help the person discover what he or she needed. Once that was completed, I was to move on. I still didn't think I knew the entirety of

Nick's story, so on every level I was failing the man I cared for most in the world.

By ten o'clock, the kids were gone, and everyone was pulling down their vehicles' decorations. Once everything was stowed in the back of the van, we drove slowly down the gravel drive to the shop.

Nick held the door open for me to enter. "Did you ladies have a busy night?" he asked.

Mother looked tired but happy. "Believe it or not, we were swamped. Not just for the free cider and popcorn balls, but folks were buying Christmas decorations."

Lillian giggled. "Good thing part of my order was in. I honestly never expected to sell anything tonight. Next year we'll have pumpkin cookies to give away. The popcorn balls were gone in the first hour. I haven't seen Francie yet, but I'm guessing this evening will be deemed a success."

They walked out with us, and Lillian turned off the light and locked the door. A couple of cars were still in the gravel lot. I heard voices, and laughter. In a moment, Miles, whom I had met at the Gypsy wagon, ran across the parking lot, chasing Matthew. Their capes were billowing out behind them in good super hero fashion.

Then the unthinkable happened. One of the cars suddenly shot forward, headed straight for Matthew. He was a few yards from me, far enough ahead of Miles that the other boy didn't seem to be in danger. I heard a scream, and started to run.

Then everything went black.

****

When I came to, my shoulder hurt like crazy, and I opened my eyes to see a crowd standing around me. Matthew's mother, Melissa, was crying.

I was afraid to say anything. I expected to feel a sudden surge of need from her.

Mother knelt next to me, kissed my forehead. "Jacqueline? Are you hurt?"

I paid attention to my body for a moment. "No. Just my shoulder. I must have hit it when I fell."

"When you *tackled* me, you mean," said a young voice.

I followed the sound and saw Matthew. His face was dirty, and his Batman costume looked like it had been in one heck of a fight. He smiled at me. "I think you saved my life, Aunt Jacquie. That girl about ran me down."

I wasn't going to explain to him that I wasn't his aunt. It was too complicated, and I liked hearing him say it. And I loved knowing he was fine.

I started to get up, with plenty of help from Melissa and the others. Then I realized Nick wasn't there.

Mother pointed toward the car that had nearly caused a disaster. "He's the Gypsy on duty."

Once I assured everyone that I was fine, the Standish family relaxed. They started saying good night and drifting toward their respective homes. Not Francie, though. The blond spitfire put her arm around my shoulders and another around Mother's, spoke words of reassurance, and predicted that by midnight, everyone in Serendipity would know of my heroism.

Lillian agreed. "You know how people are, Jacquie. Once you make a name for yourself, it sticks. I think this is going to supersede any ancient history." She looked at Mother and winked. "Don't you agree, Reba?"

"I wouldn't be surprised," Mother replied, smiling at me.

That sounded good, but I was drawn toward the car. I wanted to know what had happened, and why. Nick frowned at me as if I shouldn't interrupt, but I stood next to him and looked down at the thin girl who was sitting sideways on the car seat, her booted feet on the gravel drive, and her head in her hands. The smell of alcohol was strong. A sheriff's car was coming up the drive, and Nick explained to the girl, and the other two in the car what was going to happen next.

"Do you understand what I'm saying to you, Jasmine?" Nick asked the driver.

She nodded, and at last looked up at him and said a weak *yes.*

My breath caught, as a stab of cold pierced my heart. I saw myself in that girl. In her haunted eyes, her hopeless, sagging shoulders.

She and her friends were transferred to the

sheriff's car. As it pulled away, I looked up at Nick. His jaw was set.

"What will happen to her?" I asked.

"There are procedures. Just because Matthew wasn't hurt, doesn't mean she's not in serious trouble."

"I feel bad for her."

"I feel bad for her too, Jacquie. And Stacy, her mother. They're having a real hard time of it right now, and this won't help."

"Stacy. She works at the bank?"

He nodded, and some of the picture became clear to me. The picture of Stacy's need, Jasmine's need, and what I might do to help. And how important it was that Nick keep doing the work he loved.

"Nick, you know I wouldn't have been here tonight, if not for you, right? I would have stayed in Mother's nice, quiet house instead of braving the crowds. Jen could have brought her out, taken her home."

"Okay." Clearly, he didn't see where my line of thought was going.

"So, if not for you, Matthew might be in an

ambulance right now. Do you see that? If you believe in signs at all, if you're looking for some not-so-subtle indication that your choice of career and hometown are on the right track, try that one."

He listened carefully, not shrugging it off. "I'll think about that, Jacquie."

I cleared my throat. "And...I was thinking I should leave Serendipity right away, you know? But what's on my mind now is the ripple effect you talked about. Maybe I could do some good if I stay here. I'm a decent listener, and women like Stacy, and girls like Jasmine, need that. They need a lot of it. Maybe I could make more of a difference here than I can by hopping from place to place. There's no follow-through that way. There may be ripples, but not like here, where everybody's connected."

I laughed. "Matthew called me *Aunt Jacquie*. I feel that close to him, even though I haven't known him long."

Nick smiled, though I could tell the dangerous situation had taken a toll. "Small town is a different way of life, Aunt Jacquie."

How well I knew that. But I thought I was finally ready to risk it.

****

I drove back to Mother's, and she bid us both a quick good-night and ducked into the house. Still matchmaking, no doubt. I had to hope she succeeded.

I opened the van's back door, ready to help Nick take out decorations, and the collapsible shell created for the gypsy wagon. It was nearly midnight now, and clouds hid the moon. Just as we started to pull things out of the cargo area, the van's inside lights went out.

"Oops. Sorry about that! I'll get the carport light." I started to head that way, but Nick caught my arm.

"Just a minute. Let's leave it dark. Sets a mood." He pulled me close. I knew I should resist, but didn't. Nick ran his hands up my arms, cupped my face, and ever so gently ran his thumbs over my cheekbones. Then he took a half step closer and kissed me gently, longingly. It lasted just a moment, but felt like forever, and a tiny *something* ignited in the region of my heart.

I expected to feel the usual sensation of cold that always happened when my gift was alerted. I expected it to be more intense than usual, because with Nick it always had been. But I wasn't feeling that cold, creeping awareness. I was confused, and even though I didn't want to, tried to pull away.

Suddenly my crazy cat was in the cargo area, meowing at me worse than ever. I looked down to see what was wrong with him. Good grief, was he rolling his yellow eyes at me? Sam looked as if he wanted to tell me that I was being stupid.

Then I looked up and saw in Nick's eyes something very different.

"Nick, I'm sorry. I—I can't…"

"Sure you can, Jacquie. I don't understand why you keep pushing me away. I know you care for me. I know you want me."

"Yes. But I can't have you."

He chuckled. "You're very wrong on that."

"No. I can't… You don't understand."

"Here is what I understand. We care for each other. We always did. But since you got back to town, *bang*, there it was—stronger than ever. You would almost let me get close, then hold me off at a distance again. I wondered why, but you know what? I think I've figured it out."

"Oh. Is that right?" *Try to humor him, get out of the situation, put some distance between us and get a grip on yourself, sister.*

"Here's what I think." He pulled me even closer, so our bodies touched and I felt his words on my forehead as he spoke. "I think you just don't want to admit that you need me. Pretty simple. You're an independent lady, used to doing everything your way, living by your own agenda. You don't want to admit that, deep down, there's one tiny thing missing from your life. And for some reason, I think that one thing is *me*." He stroked my hair, rubbed my back. "I think I'm pretty lucky to be what you need. Makes me feel special."

I held my breath. He was right. The sensation I'd been having since I arrived had been more intense than usual because *I was sensing the hole in my own soul*, and I'd been thrown right into the arms of the answer. I needed love and companionship, laughs and hugs.

That little fire that had seemed to ignite inside me had really been the missing piece of my soul finding its place. What a warm, delicious feeling. I sighed, leaning my head on Nick's shoulder.

I smiled to myself, feeling beautiful, radiant and happy. Very, very happy.

Sam plopped down in the back of the van and began to purr. It almost seemed like he'd known this was the way our story would turn out.

The End...

Or is it The Beginning?

Epilogue

IT TOOK SOME time and patience, as most worthwhile things do, but Nick and I have created a life in Serendipity that feels as if it was meant to be.

He's chief of police, and I've learned to be flexible around his erratic schedule. Like Carla Standish, I travel for work. Sometimes I'm gone for a week or more, but occasionally, when the destination is near enough, Nick is able to take off, and go with me.

When I'm home, I run a tiny coffee house on the town square. Jamison Kincaid and his wife Darlene had bought the miniscule storefront, and hadn't decided what to do with it. When I mentioned my wish to have a place where people could just sit and visit, vent if they needed to, in a relaxed atmosphere, Darlene was surprisingly agreeable. Evidently her *perfect children* had been through their own rough years, and she saw the need for such a venue in Serendipity. It was another reminder that we're not aware of what others are going through, simply by knowing them on a casual level.

From opening day, Jasmine was one of my regular customers, and now she works for me a few hours a week, after school. She and I share stories, tears, and the satisfaction of knowing we're both working through difficulties we didn't think we could survive.

Once Nick and I were together, and I was whole, I felt confident enough to tell him the truth about my gift. He took it completely in stride, and came up with the idea for the coffee house.

I love living next door to Mother, and five minutes from Jen. And Matthew Standish still calls me Aunt Jacquie.

I wouldn't have it any other way. We're all family here in Serendipity. The ripples are never-ending.

A Note From the Author

Thank you so very much for reading Jacqueline and Nick's story!

Years ago, I wrote A PIECE OF HER SOUL as a short story, and it was published in a little Halloween collection. I think the whole thing was eight pages long.

But when I started planning the Serendipity, Indiana series, I knew I wanted to turn those eight pages into something more. I hope you enjoyed Jacquie and Nick's journey. Isn't it interesting that they found what they needed right where they began years ago?

How often do we search in vain for happiness and fulfillment, only to realize it was within our grasp the entire time? How often do we see the behavior of people around us, and make quick judgments, instead of trying to understand what is going on in the background? And how often do we expect people to conform to our expectations, instead of letting them follow their own purpose?

I always love to hear from readers. You can email me through the contact box on my website:

http://www.magdalenascott.com.

I also send a monthly-*ish* newsletter. To sign up for that, enter your email in the form on this page: http://www.magdalenascott.com/p/contact.html

Until we meet again—Happy Reading!

Magdalena

For Free Reads, Sneak Previews & backstage info, become a Newsletter Subscriber!

I love to connect with readers! Please sign up for my newsletter so we can stay in touch. Don't worry about me clogging up your email inbox—I only send an email if I have actual news to share. The sign-up form is on my website. Just type into your browser: http://www.magdalenascott.com/p/contact.html

Also in the Serendipity, Indiana, series:

SMALL TOWN CHRISTMAS

Melissa is moving back to Serendipity, Indiana to raise her young son and run her new business—in spite of a painful past and the fact that her ex-boyfriend still lives in their hometown.

EMILY'S DREAMS

Emily Kincaid has a second chance at life, and a voice in her head that keeps nudging her along. But she can't move forward without dealing with her past.

CHRISTMAS WEDDING

Dec. 1: Jim Standish is ready—right this minute—to marry the love of his life, but Melissa Singer wants the day to be one they'll look back on forever. Planning and execution time: 25 days. Will it be possible to create the perfect Christmas Wedding?

THE BLANK BOOK

Alice Williams is surviving widowhood, but must unlock the secrets of a mysterious blank book before she can confidently step into her future with a man she's afraid to love.

THE RING

Happily-ever-after is out of the question. But in Serendipity, the Magic of Love does amazing things.

THE ROAD NOT TAKEN

Francie Standish Carrington has some tough decisions to make, and a lot of questions about a past she thought she understood.

A PIECE OF HER SOUL

Jacqueline needs a break from the constant strain of the special gift she has. But the little cottage on a quiet street isn't quite the retreat she expected, due to the presence of a handsome next door neighbor.

ONCE UPON A TIME

Taylor Kincaid has big plans for her life, and falling in love with the mysterious new shop owner in her hometown isn't one of them. Sweet romance, "coincidences" that might be more than that, and a love that survives the unthinkable come together in this new Serendipity, Indiana tale.

A COWBOY FOR CHRISTMAS

Hannah Kincaid has her eye on Jacob Hollingsworth, the handsome co-owner of Serendipity's new (and only) dude ranch. When Jacob's brother Michael shows up, everything at the Rocking H is turned on its head-- including Hannah's plans.

Magdalena's Legend, Tennessee Titles

MIDNIGHT IN LEGEND, TN

CHRISTMAS COLLISION

WHERE HER HEART IS

BUILDING A DREAM

SECOND CHANCES

CHRISTMAS CHARM

HOME FOR CHRISTMAS

UNDER THE MISTLETOE (Prequel)

THE HOLLY AND THE IVY (Prequel)